BULLIES

ON

JUICE

A Novel

GEORGE ONSTOT

ISBN: 0988157101
ISBN-13: 978-0988157101
Published by The Good Word
710 7th Avenue
New Westminster, British Columbia V3M 5V3

DEDICATION

This is dedicated to the people of Bayporte, Great Elizabeth, Canada. The Bayporters are beautiful, and so is their province. I know this because I created them that way.

"WINNING ISN'T EVERYTHING; IT'S THE ONLY THING."

VINCE LOMBARDI

1

I kept nodding off and daydreaming in Vlad Rybka's Hummer when Vlad finally reached his destination in the middle of nowhere. We had been going north of Bayporte for over an hour on the crumbling Western Canadian Highway. Vlad, Barrie Weston and Pavel Pavlovich were sitting in the front, practically in each other's lap. I had volunteered to sit in the back, where I could stretch out and close my eyes.

The Hummer slowed, then stopped. Pavel fell out, laughing uproariously, followed by the rest of us. He had a bottle of Canadian Comfort. "Here, superstar," he said, tossing the bottle at me. "Drink some. Make man of you. Put hair on your cock."

Normally, I liked to stay indoors on such raw days. But today I'd traveled into the Canadian wilderness with three rowdy hockey players. I needed to be a good sport.

"Shit, man! Look!" Vlad shouted as he stood urinating. A couple of fat pheasants swung past us on the brisk wind. "Where my gun?"

"They're too far away now," I said.

"Who got my focking gun?" he yelled.

I handed him his rifle. He fired away, his ammunition disappearing into the endless sky with a startling crackle and a faint whiff of gunpowder.

Other pheasants flew from the trees and past us. The three guys went ahead towards the taller trees. I got my discount-store rifle and trailed them.

"They will come back," said Vlad. "When they do, we kill them dead." He laughed. "Kill them dead. Them focking birds."

A small bird fluttered by and the two big Russians fired at once. All I saw was a sprinkling of feathers after the shooting was done.

Pavel laughed. "See? What we tell you? They fly by, they die."

Barrie Weston looked over his shoulder at me and winked. I had come out here with these guys as a favor to Barrie. He said it would be good for morale, though he didn't say whose morale. Vlad and Pavel, our teammates, were ambivalent about me, and I nearly pissed my pants whenever they looked in my direction. They intimidated me plenty in the locker room, but out here, drunk and armed, they were truly terrifying. Barrie and I had a tacit understanding that he would intervene if these big Russians tried to kill me.

Pavel and Vlad walked out in front of Barrie and me. "Something wrong?" Barrie asked.

"My ass is sore from my last injection," I said.

"So is mine." Weston, our team captain, had the unshakable, unflappable calm that most great leaders seemed to possess. "Just let them have these guys have their fun and everything will be fine."

"Maybe *they* should start juicing, too."

He chuckled. "They don't need it. They're crazy enough already. Stay out of their way, that's all."

"I'll do my best."

We heard their shotguns and laughter again, but nothing hit the ground.

"My hit! My hit!" Pavel yelled.

"Bullshit! You didn't hit nothing! I got it!" Vlad yelled back.

"You both missed, guys," I said. I felt glad they missed, especially because Pavel once put a wounded bird out of its misery by decapitating it with his fingers. Then he threw it at me.

We kept walking along and our luck improved or worsened, I wasn't sure which. The big guys shot four or five pheasants. Weston and I even shot one or two, and Vlad spotted an owl staring stupidly at us, so he blew it away. To celebrate, he drank some more Canadian Comfort and we all sat on rocks and gazed out at the northern wilderness for a few minutes. Vlad drew his weapon and aimed at a few geese on the water. He shot four or five, and when two became airborne, Weston shot one.

Pavel laughed. "I hit two with one bullet!"

Weston shook his head. "That's easy when they're both sitting on the water."

"They were getting ready to fly!" Pavel laughed harder.

"What do we do with all these dead birds?" I asked.

"Leave them here," Vlad said. "You want to eat bird for dinner, go to restaurant. Here, we shoot them and leave them for wildlife to eat. We have no license. Cops bust us if they catch us."

Wilderness, I thought. Someday, I might like to leave the crazy city of Bayporte and settle down out here. But not yet. For the time being, I belonged to the city.

"Are you having fun?" Weston muttered to me. "Say it to yourself: 'I am having fun.'"

I saw a bald eagle way up high, floating on the rugged winds of the magnificent Canadian sky. The two big Russians blasted away. I looked up and saw the eagle still up there, probably unaware that two maniacs were trying to kill it.

"Dammit!" Weston yelled. "No killing an eagle, you hear me? Eagles are off limits!"

Pavel and Vlad nodded, chuckling. Dead birds in the water and of dead birds on the ground, all because of us. I hoped some animal would enjoy eating them, since I felt all right about killing another creature for food. We waited in vain for a while for other birds to fly by, then returned to the Hummer. Vlad, angry that we had run out of Canadian Comfort, ordered me to drive while Weston sat next to me and the Russians rode on the vehicle's front bumper. We crept along the road and Barrie reminded me of what he'd said about being a good sport and having a good time. "Yes," he said, "you can find plenty of reasons to feel good if you make the effort."

I heard shotguns go off again.

"You got him!" Pavel said. "You shot his ass. Ouch! How will he shit now?"

"Is his problem, not mine!" Vlad replied.

A large black cat was struggling along without a tail or hind paws. Weston shook his head while I slowed the Hummer. Weston drew his weapon and blasted the cat away, ending its misery. He looked at where the cat had lain, then he glowered at his laughing teammates. "Dammit, what did I tell you? If you hit it, kill it. There's enough suffering in the world already." Sighing, he put his gun away and I put my foot on the gas pedal.

"Maniacs. Psychopaths. Head cases," I said. "It's hard for me to have fun when they're drunk and armed."

"We're just about done for today," Weston said.

Soon after, Pavel and Vlad got black inside the Hummer and put away their guns. We headed back to Bayporte and reached the pancake house where we had parked our vehicles.

"I'll ride in with Cross," Weston said. "We'll meet up with you at Bourdin's party later on." They nodded at him and snarled at me.

The late-afternoon wind blew hard and cold. Canadians accept the cold, harsh days and savor the clear, mild ones. I love Bayporte on a flawless spring day; she's like a pretty girl, all made up, smiling in the sunshine.

Sometimes, Bayporte drives me bananas. The new people from overseas have made our city their own, demolishing most of what was old and replacing it with glittering monuments to capitalist enterprise. Some of these immigrants, with their third-grade English, own lavish West Shore estates with priceless views of the Tyson River and northern mountains. I've read that many of these zillionaires are ambivalent about our boring Bayporte and wish to return to Hong Kong. Some folks just don't know a good thing.

Weston and I drove along in my brand-new black BMW.

'You need a new car, eh? Go to the dealer, the top guy,' Barrie had said. 'Tell him I sent you. He's a friend of a friend, and he'll get you the best deal around.'

The top guy, too busy to see me, palmed me off on one of his flunkies, who probably got me the same deal he got everyone else. I had wanted simple, reliable transportation; instead, I got an oversized, shiny black phallus of a car whose interior reeked of fine leather. It came with Sirius and XM satellite radio and a GPS. A lady with a sexy voice told me where to turn.

"Where's the ganja, mon? It make Canada beautiful," Weston said. "Especially after a day of hunting."

"Barrie, your Jamaican accent just don't cut it, mon. Just call it pot like everyone else, OK?"

"Need to have that ganja to make me feel so good. Got to have that Bob Marley or Jimmy Cliff reggae music, too, mon."

"We're not supposed to smoke while we're using steroids. But if you insist, check the glove box."

I scanned the satellite radio stations for some reggae music. When Weston started talking like that, I half expected him to suddenly grow dreadlocks and turn black. He lit the doobie and took a long hit, then passed it to me.

"It's *so* good, mon. " He added, "It's not as good as warm, wet pussy, but what is?"

Barrie and I had toked up in public washrooms and bars. Not long ago, while flying home from Quebec, Weston and I crept into the lavatory together. Just as we exited, the flight attendant passed by, immediately assaulted by a ripe fog of cannabis smoke. She just shook her head, like, "Please, gentlemen, not here, on *my* flight..."

We drove up to the bridge toll booth. Down below, the Tyson River raged, beautiful and treacherous. I stopped, rolled down my window and handed the man exact change. Fiftyish, paunchy and preoccupied with swallowing the last bite of his lunch, he wore a name tag saying James Hall.

Weston leaned over towards my window and said, "Hey, James, how's it goin'? How's the family?"

James frowned a bit, as if being ridiculed, then looked closer and saw one of the most famous faces in Canadian sports. Like a true hockey freak, he nearly choked on his mouthful of food as he smiled and waved us through.

"Friend of yours?" I asked.

Barrie let out a little pot giggle. "No, I just saw his name and decided to make his day. He'll remember that moment for the rest of his life."

We sped across the bridge and zoomed along towards downtown. Bayporte. Before World War Two, much of the city had been scrubland, but now magazines called Bayporte the ultimate urban playground, full of gleaming buildings, nightclubs and clothing boutiques. A nice place to visit, but most Bayporters could scarcely afford to live here.

"Take this joint!" Barrie ordered. "No more for me."

I accepted it. "Jacques wants to see me tomorrow morning."

"Maybe he's going to give you a raise."

"No. He's got something else on his mind."

"Maybe he'll surprise you." Weston paused. "That was quite a goal you scored last game. Couldn't have come at a better time."

I grinned. "Yeah, it *was* pretty fucking awesome."

"You keep playing like that and you'll end up in the Hall of Fame."

"We'll be inducted together," I said.

"Sounds good," he replied, "as long as we don't get busted first for juicing."

We both fell silent. Finally I said, "You and I should go into business together. We're both celebrities."

"What kind of business?"

"We could open a strip joint together. We could meet and greet people at the door and hand out condoms and Kleenex."

"Listen, Cross, I don't want to compromise my wholesome image."

I hooted. "Barrie, you could open a brothel and I don't think it would surprise anyone."

He didn't like that. We didn't speak again for several minutes.

"Do you have plans for after you retire?" I asked.

"Do *you?*"

"Sometimes. I've given it thought, but I'm not ready to retire just yet."

"Me neither," he said. "You should have respect for Jacques. He's our boss."

"So I guess we have to kiss his ass."

"See? That's what I mean. Don't get an attitude," Weston said.

"It's a free country. Do your own thing." I did a quick imitation of Barrie. "'Hey, kids, I'm Barrie Weston. I'm here to give you a few tips on living a good life. Take steroids and chase women. Put on your skates, get on the ice and give someone a concussion. Try it, you'll like it.'"

"Fuck you, Crossley."

I laughed and turned off the reggae music. I settled on a Doors song and smiled. The Doors and driving went together well. The Doors went well with everything.

"Wouldn't it be fun," Weston said, "if, in the off season, we drove down to the southern States and went into all those honkytonks they sing about it country songs? The ones with the best music and the worst women." He closed his eyes and smiled. "Party every night. Dance my ass off, fuck my brains out."

"Sounds like a good way to get your ass kicked by someone's jealous boyfriend," I said.

"Life is short, so you have to live it to the fullest. Pain and pleasure. Winning and losing. Births and deaths. It's all one big cycle, man." He nodded. "Live fast, love hard, die young."

I thought of a trip we had taken down the West Coast. We filled the car with gas and drove to Los Angeles, stopping only to piss. We stayed at some tacky joint that *Entertainment Tonight* called Hollywood's hippest hotel. In the middle of the night, Weston laid the night clerk in the ostentatious lobby. I watched them go at it until I got bored and went upstairs to watch TV. The night clerk, an aging pretty woman, had probably moved to Los Angeles twenty years earlier to try breaking into movies. While she and Weston were pumping away, she told him that her son was a hockey fan who would be thrilled if, after their fucking, Weston would pose for a cell phone picture with her. On the way back to Bayporte, Weston talked about his sex life, babbling about every woman he had ever mounted.

"I'm still young," he said now, "and have many big decisions to make. I want to stay young and be productive. Isn't that the right way to look at things?"

"Absolutely. There *is* life after hockey." I accelerated and looked up at the Bayporte skyline. I liked cities' downtowns in general, even this one, though it didn't have much history, tragedy or scandal to boast of. I drove past downtown, to the lovely community of West Shore, and reached Bourdin's house. Weston got out and took a piss on the hedges. I admired how he could do that with all the voices nearby, the people who were likely to see him, the cops who would have ticketed him. I trailed Weston so that I could watch his entrance to

Bourdin's party. He stood in the doorway, his hands clasped together in prayer as he addressed the room.

"For the Bullies to win the Stanley Cup this year, we pray to the Lord." His deep voice boomed for all to hear.

"Lord hear our prayer," someone called back.

Everybody laughed, and Barrie waded into an ocean of hugs, kisses and high fives. I waited until the crowd had gone back inside, then slipped in and made a place for myself on the kitchen counter. I could see just about everyone and everything from there. I had seen most of those people at other parties but didn't actually know many of them except my teammates.

Vlad and Pavel sat ogling some woman's big breasts. She didn't seem to mind, and I wondered if she would get angry once they started grabbing them. Mark Ignas, the handsome Native forward from some reservation in Ontario, sat on a sofa in the living room, checking it all out. A remarkable athlete, Ignas reminded me of Jim Thorpe, but our team's coaches, management and players considered him rude and aloof. Whenever local reporters asked him about being

Canada's premier Native athlete, he just shrugged and said, "Well, in Nineteen-seventy-three, Wounded Knee happened…"

Jacques didn't like flippant players and would have traded him if Ignas hadn't been so damned good.

I sat by myself in a corner of the kitchen. Soon a man and woman came in. He wore a garish pink shirt, khaki slacks and a salon tan. She, a pretty blonde in her early twenties, wept into a Kleenex.

"Aren't you being a bit hard on him?" the man asked her.

"Donny's a jerk. I don't want to see him again."

"Give him a second chance," he said.

"No way. He's a prick. No more Donny Bourdin for me, Sean." She saw me and looked away. He looked at me and offered me a handshake. "Sean Marcelin. We've met. You were at Donny's last party."

I shook his hand but wondered about the girl. I looked past him and stared at her some more.

"This is Angela," Sean said. "She's mad at Donny. She'll get over it.

Cross, you play great hockey. What's your secret?"

"If I had a secret, do you think I'd tell *you*?"

He chuckled. "Look, Angela needs me right now. But let me give you my card. Call me when you get the chance. I have some investment opportunities you'll be interested in." He reached into his wallet, withdrew his card and handed it to me. "We'll do some business and pick up some sweeties." He left and I tore up his card.

Our host, the celebrated Donny Bourdin, stood apart from the others, talking to our teammate and his best friend, Denis Pilon, a defenseman from Quebec. Both were tall, muscular, handsome men in a steroids sort of way. Suddenly Donny gave Denis's face the lightest slap, and Denis doubled over, his face red with merriment.

As soon as Pilon straightened up, Bourdin started up with the play-slaps again. They began a brotherly slapping contest, both smiling but slapping harder each time. Their faces grew darker, but they kept on smiling. Just then Bourdin, his face quivering and chest heaving, tackled Pilon and the two went crashing into the coffee table. The two big men lay there on the floor in an utterly exhausted embrace.

Then one kissed the other on the lips, and the other one seemed to kiss back harder, as if this, too, were a competition.

"Yuck!" Angela turned her face away from the spectacle. "They make me want to puke."

"You just don't understand about male bonding," said Sean.

The kiss ended and the two hockey players got up.

"Cross," Donny said, coming over and shaking my hand, "nice of you to join us. Did you bring a sweetie? No? Well, let me get you one." He disappeared into his roomful of guests.

Donny's party, well into its fourth or fifth hour, seemed, if anything, to gain momentum. Hockey parties were fun. Professional hockey players party harder than other folks. The players practice and lift weights, then suit up, get on the ice and virtually try to kill their opponents to get control of the puck. They unwound, or maybe just came undone, at these gatherings.

Some of these parties, surprisingly, included wives. The spectacle of a marital fight in public always fascinated me. I had witnessed, and participated in, my share of spats, and they convinced me that getting divorced was the most intelligent, if expensive, thing I had ever done. Hockey husbands fought harder, and dirtier, at home than on the ice; their wives, while screaming profanities, threw things at them and tried to knock them cold.

During our brief, ignominious marriage, my wife had tried to remake me into the kind of man she wanted. She and some other hockey wives tried to end our parties on the grounds that they had grown weary of watching their spouses behave like swine as the whole world watched. I didn't know what "whole world" they meant; we acted like swine only around each other and our wives.

Eventually, I came to understand that the wives happily bonded with each other in their efforts to break up our parties. The men did the same thing, sort of; we formed intense relationships—one could not always call them friendships—in locker rooms, training camps and long airline trips. We often got to know each other better than our wives ever could know us, and had no problem about withholding from our women the things we said during our all-male bull sessions. Our wives had baby showers, card games, Tupperware parties and—sometimes—evenings out to whistle at male strippers.

During their girl-power celebrations, they would exchange gossip, truths, half-truths and flat-out lies about their men, to be used against us in the bedroom, naked and priapic, or as we packed up for road trips, hurried and preoccupied.

"Jaylene Weston said Barrie spent Tuesday night at home. Were *you* off screwing some hockey groupie?" my missus had demanded to know once.

Our women wanted to be married to gentlemen, not swine. Over time, they took over some of our parties and altered them to their own personal tastes. One Halloween, I arrived home after a devastating overtime loss to some team we should have pounded. My wife stood in the living room, wearing a Wonder Woman costume. She and the other team wives had arranged a party at a downtown hotel, about which I had altogether forgotten.

"You need to get into this." She thrust at me a Superman costume. Her status among the hockey wives, a crucial matter to *her*, depended largely upon *my* success with the Bayporte Bullies; and at that particular time, her husband, a man of 'unfulfilled potential,' just couldn't seem to stop screwing up.

"No," I said. "I won't put it on."

I had spent that afternoon sweating, straining, hitting and losing in a far-off city, then hurrying to catch a plane back home. So I refused to go downtown dressed as Superman so my teammates could all laugh at me.

"You're so selfish." She whimpered. "You won't go along with anything. I promised everyone we would be there."

"I am not going to the Marriott, or wherever the hell it is, dressed like a comic book faggot."

"You have to go. I promised everyone we'd be there." She reached back and down, pulling a bit of costume out of her ass crack.

"I'm tired, dear heart. I failed in front of thousands of people hours ago." I had the puck, in front of the other team's mostly empty net, but I missed the shot. I could have tied the game.

"You always cop some excuse when *I* want to do something, but you can always find the energy to go with your hockey pals." She sighed and adjusted her mask. "I just want to do things like normal people."

I fell back on my usual excuse. "We aren't normal. We're special. When my hockey days are over, we won't be special anymore and we can do normal things."

"You're so unwilling to compromise." Her face grew sweaty, her costume uncomfortable. "You probably regret marrying me."

She loved hurling such verbal barbs at me. She had started antagonizing me after we got married because of a pregnancy that soon became a miscarriage. *Did* I regret marrying her? Sometimes, but even *I* wasn't stupid enough to say so. I assured her of my delight in being her husband. But she called me a liar and could always find new ways of accusing me of having failed her.

Or, even worse, accusing herself of having failed me.

Later, I wondered if I had been too slow to comfort her, or maybe I wanted to make her mad. I paused a bit too long before reassuring her of my undying love.

"No, I don't regret marrying you at all," I said.

"Asshole!"

She ran into the bathroom and threw open the medicine chest; suicide attempts were her favorite means of retaliation. Always horrified by blood, she took pills as an alternative to cutting herself. Afraid of killing herself, she took just enough pills to make herself goofy for a day or so.

I headed towards the bedroom, exhausted and dispirited. The puck on my stick had looked up at me, as if saying, "Here I am, Cross. There's the net. *Do it!*"

"Motherfucker!" she screamed, unable to get the safety cap off the pill bottle. "You don't care what happens to me! Burn in hell, you dickhead!"

I hung my head and sighed. The puck had been right there. I tried to slap it in but missed. I whiffed, period.

I went to the bathroom and discovered that my wife had started breaking things. As brutal a fighter as any man, she probably wanted to punch me out for trying to humor her. I wanted her to work me over as punishment for missing that fucking puck.

I went into the living room and saw her sitting on the floor, looking at old pictures of us. "Can you ever forgive me?" she asked.

I chuckled. Bad idea, chuckling at my missus.

She stripped off her Wonder Woman costume, grabbed mine from the kitchen table, and stormed outside. Stuffing the pile of colorful, fire-retardant garments into our metal garbage can, she dropped in a lighted match. She stood there in her brassiere and underpants, watching the blaze with a pyromaniac's fascination.

I didn't know what to do about her. Or about us.

The fire seemed to pacify her a little bit. Within minutes we were driving to the party, both of us dressed in tidy, casual, totally inappropriate attire.

"I'm sorry," I said.

She said nothing.

"I apologize for that scene back there," I added. "I don't know why I said those things."

"You always say something like that after we fight. You go play hockey and then come home and zone out in front of the TV set. Or you go chasing whores with Barrie." She added, "Let's have a child."

"Let's wait till I'm done with hockey. Then we'll have two." That fucking puck had been right on my stick and I blew it. How often do you get such an easy chance to score in the NHL? Shitfuck!

"With you it's just hockey, hockey, hockey."

"The hockey pays our bills, sweetness. You want to try making some money for a while?" I had been right in front of a practically empty net, just me and Mr. Puck. How did I manage to botch that up?

"Maybe I *should* start a career. It might do my self-esteem some good." She had volunteered as a public relations assistant at a charity for a while until the office manager fired her. I thought that was weird, to be fired from a job where they weren't even paying you. She had bought a dozen business suits for that unsalaried position, and her fancy new wardrobe now hung in our closet, zippered up in nylon bags.

"Chris," she said as we got closer to the hotel, "you should get more motivated to do those promotional kinds of things. Barrie's always on TV or the radio, selling stuff." I had declined opportunities for meet-and-greet work and other personal appearances due to my deep desire not to shake strangers' hands and kiss their bums.

Son of a bitch, I couldn't believe I missed that puck. Jacques probably didn't like it too much, either.

"I see Vlad on TV sometimes, selling condoms. His English is getting better." She added, "Jayleen Weston says you and Barrie are getting stoned all the time."

"Jayleen is a lying cunt." Barrie and I tried to get our wives to smoke pot with us, but they freaked out about prison terms and mental illness. My wife practically sniffed me like a cop dog sometimes. I must have been too greedy when I got the puck and whiffed it. The little fucker was right on my stick.

We reached the Marriott ballroom. Everyone else had arrived in costume. I told them my wife and I had come dressed as bored suburbanites. They all laughed and probably guessed that we'd just had one hell of a marital row and destroyed our costumes. She went to sit with the other and wives, some tricked out as whores or dominatrices. I got a drink and sat alone for a while, largely ignored as a party pooper by the other men. Vlad Rybka, dressed as a Nazi, made everyone howl with his straight-armed salutes and ludicrous German accent: "Ze fuhrer vas busy, so he zent me!" Barrie came dressed as a cowboy, pointing his six-shooters and saying, "Bang, bang! You're still alive, but roll over and play dead!"

By the end of the night I had gotten falling-down drunk. After staggering to our car, I slept in the back seat while my wife drove. I woke up when we reached home and she killed the engine. "Loser," she said, reaching over and slapping my face. She got out and marched into our house. I remembered that she had all the keys, so I had nowhere to go. Fortunately, drunkenness made me very warm and sleepy, so I curled up for the night and slept in the car.

At Donny Bourdin's party, I wandered into his bedroom, a designer pigsty with Versace bedclothes rumpled and stiff, and a flat-screen Sony TV hanging askew on one wall. A black iPad sat on one pillow, and credit cards of every color lay scattered on his nightstand like a drunkard's poker hand. He bought whatever he wanted, whenever he wanted it. The bank managers shook his hand and insisted on posing with him for cell phone pictures. On Donny's walls were framed pictures of Barbara Charlton, a fresh-faced Northup University coed majoring in Being the Best I Can Be. Barbara, always striving to overcome her lustful feelings, regretted premarital sex with Donny but rode his dick on most weekends. Donny regretted nothing; he delighted in driving his repressed girl to screaming, thrashing orgasms. Barbara, naturally, stayed away from our parties. Donny, according to their agreement, would just say no to the hockey groupies and say yes to monogamy once he'd decided to settle down with Barbara.

I sat on his bed for a moment and started searching through his dresser drawers for his stash of weed. We had stopped using harder recreational drugs once we started with performance-enhancing ones. In this very bedroom, Bourdin, eager to build muscle on his lanky, skinny frame, had stood naked while I turned him on to steroids. He had become prodigiously muscular, a proficient self-injector and vastly better hockey player. All of us juicers could train for countless hours and, on the ice, race for and control the puck with a stamina and singlemindedness that awed the crowd and frustrated the opposition.

I smoked some of Bourdin's grass and thought back over the past few years. Like Donny, I had been a scrawny youngster whose body stubbornly refused to respond to its regimen of diet and exercise. I could scarcely remember desiring anything from life except a spot on the Bullies' roster. Perhaps only good fortune allowed me, a decent but anything-but-great Northup Grizzlies forward, to become a Bayporte Bullies draft selection. As a pro, I had played my best, and sometimes even better. Unfortunately, I could rarely completely satisfy Jacques and the fear lingered over my head like a pall of smoke that he would demote me to second line or release me altogether.

I stubbed out the joint and lay down on Donny's bed. My eyes traveled about the room, to his big-screen TV and Mac desktop computer that still had its cellophane wrapping. My mind refused to settle down, and I pictured, on Donny's TV and computer screens, gray-haired talking heads going on about the dangers of steroids and human growth hormones.

The steroids saved me. I developed muscle, strength and stamina, enough to manhandle any defenseman. I played with such resilience that I swore I had grown a third lung. Soon, Bourdin and the others were juicing, too. We used them and spoke to each other about dosages and cycles with an expert's precision. We needed to keep our mouths shut if we wished to continue using the drugs and enjoying their benefits.

Jacques doubtless had come to consider me an ineffectual body checker and a pitiful wimp when battling for the puck in front of the net. After convincing myself that my teammate Wally Horton would replace me on the first line, I thought I might have a nervous breakdown. But no; good things happened. Ideally, the good things would continue.

After separating from my wife, I had removed my wedding band. I lifted my left hand now and imagined, on my ring finger, the NHL championship ring I expected to own: a beautiful, chunky item of black onyx, white gold and tiny diamonds quite cleverly fashioned into a gleaming piece of art. The Bullies, by no coincidence, wore the NFL Oakland Raiders' colors; the steely-eyed, square-jawed tough guy on our uniforms looked like the Raiders' pirate minus his eye patch.

At times I wondered, when I thought of the championship ring I coveted, what good team success was if we didn't feel like a team. When an athlete, regardless of his sport, team or nation, comes to realize that everyone is potentially his enemy, he begins to understand the true nature and spirit of competitive sports. His teammates this year may be his opponents next year; this year's fans may be booing him next season. The only real fan, friend and teammate he will ever have is himself.

Sports teams are just a temporary collection of people wearing the same uniforms; playing for Jacques convinced me of that. To him, team success and personal success were one and the same. But winning itself, for the team or its fans, did not mean very much to him; he cared only about how good it made him look. When Weston, Bourdin, Ignas and the rest of us failed to make Jacques look good, he would dispense with us immediately.

I went back to the living room to rejoin the party. Mark Ignas still sat on one of the sofas. I plopped down next to him and said, my voice quiet, "Do you need anything from Simon?"

"I'm fixed for the time being," he muttered. "Get a new connection. Simon is too damned expensive."

"I have a meeting with Jacques in the morning. I'll see Simon soon, too."

Ignas grinned. "I wonder what Jacques wants to talk about."

"I'm going in there and sign a full confession and implicate all you guys, too."

He shook his head. "Don't even joke about shit like that. I've had meetings with him, too. He wants to know why I'm so good and can skate all day and half the night without getting winded. So I tell him, 'Well, Coach, I'm a hard-working young Native who eats right and takes vitamins.' Jacques, Roderick and Gotcha are getting pretty paranoid. Hope they don't make us do a piss test."

"We have ways of getting around that. Let's just keep playing good hockey and win a few Stanley Cups." I got up and saw people dancing outside by the pool.

Pavel stood in the middle of the living room in his underwear. He had found a small Nerf football and threw it at people's heads, then demanded they return it to him so he could throw it some more. Nobody liked being beaned by him, and everyone ducked as the orange foam toy sailed through the room, but we all tried to look upon his antics as just good fun. Whoever got conked on the head laughed and rubbed his head, which seemed to be the only option when the person throwing the ball made his living by beating up on other men.

I loitered in the kitchen and watched the party, as one might observe a frenzied herd of animals on the African plain. Three girls sat together on a sofa, legs crossed and eyes wide, almost certainly Canadian Airways flight attendants who had been conjoined at the hips since their training program in Saskatchewan. They appeared at once thrilled to be at a Bullies' party, yet conscious of the airline's admonition not to fuck any passengers. A slim girl in corduroy slacks and a black T-shirt sat next to Ignas, and she looked the most desirable, but from her body language she clearly wanted him. The only one left, Pat Paterson's pretty date, sat alone, perhaps wishing to be somewhere else.

The scion of an affluent Canadian mining family, Paterson had become a successful nightclub operator scarcely out of college. Lately he had completed a two-month stay recuperating at Peaceful Village

GEORGE ONSTOT

after the Bayporte police caught him at West Side Mall, naked and brandishing a firearm, saying he was going to assassinate Celine Dion. The cops took him away and the doctors sent him out to Peaceful Village, where they smoothed him out on Zoloft and trazedone until his recent discharge.

Paterson and Bourdin had spent many chummy evenings together joyriding in Paterson's cars, drinking Hennessy brandy, talking on their cell phones and pointing Paterson's .357 Magnum at terrified pedestrians. Paterson often carried a firearm, and apparently ignored the Canadian cops' and courts' orders to leave his weapons at a gun club. Although Paterson's mania sometimes unnerved Bourdin, the two men remained close friends and were always welcome at each other's home.

Like Sean Marcelin, Paterson frequently provided sexy women who wanted to party with the Bayporte Bullies. Paterson and Marcelin also constantly wanted to do business with the well-paid people they met. At that moment, Paterson pointed and made faces at Barrie Weston as the money man rambled on about everything from international terrorism to why movie theatres topped their popcorn with vegetable oil instead of butter. Barrie nodded and shrugged but endured this conversation, the way most of us indulge rich people.

I went over to Paterson's date, a pretty woman sitting alone for the moment.

"Are you thirsty?" I asked her.

She smiled. "A Diet Coke would be nice."

"Coming up." I went into the kitchen, wondering why a teetotaler had come here. Denis Pilon stood by the refrigerator, punching himself in the eye. His eyelid started turning blue and yellow.

"Denis," I said, "don't do that."

"I have to," he replied, "because a pretty stew in there is a total hockey freak." He hit himself some more. "She saw the bruise on my stomach and looked like she was gonna come right then. So if I show her some real damage, she'll probably let me in her pants." He smiled and punched himself a few more times.

"Denis," I said, "you're an idiot."

"Maybe. But I get more pussy in one week than you get in a whole year." He certainly did. His face, flushed and sweaty, began to swell up. People said that Denis took uppers, downers, laughers, screamers. I had personally injected him enough times to turn his ass into a pincushion.

He went off with a hugely triumphant smile, and I looked around for a clean glass but could find none; I could not even find dish soap to wash off a dirty glass. In the refrigerator I found a cold, unopened can of Diet Coke, so I wiped it off and took it in to my nice new lady friend in the living room. I wanted to take her home with me, but she'd come with Paterson and that made her unavailable to me unless she said otherwise.

"No glass?" she asked as I handed her the can of pop.

"His glasses are a health hazard. You would need a shot of penicillin afterwards."

"Lovely." She rubbed at the can's top with her sleeve and opened it. "At least it's cold."

"My name is Chris Crossley," I said. "People call me Cross."

"Laurel English," she said. "People call me Laurel."

"Hello, Laurel." I shook her hand and didn't want to give it back. "Want to go somewhere else?"

"No, I came with a date."

"Dump him," I suggested.

"Just like that?" she asked.

I paused. "I'm used to getting what I want."

"I'm sure," she said. "I have an early day tomorrow. I'm going home soon."

"You can't leave," I said. "I haven't finished charming you."

"You haven't started."

"Let me tell you about myself. I graduated from Northup and have no STDs. I have lost teeth and bought new ones, like most NHL players. I am not and never have been a Communist."

"Well," she said, "that makes you far more interesting than I am. I brush my teeth obsessively and have never had a cavity. I have considered both a rhinoplasty and boob job but have procrastinated on both. I don't go to parties much."

Just then we heard noises from somewhere else in the house.

"Vlad! Behave yourself!" Sean Marcelin, the rich man who wanted to use other people's money to make himself richer, shouted at Vlad to quit being lewd with Marcelin's date. Nona Farley, a Miss Bayporte runner-up, stood red-faced with embarrassment as Vlad clutched her hips in simulated intercourse. Marcelin, trying to separate them, succeeded only in annoying Vlad. He pumped faster and laughed louder; his eyes narrowed as he looked down at the small, pinkish male fingers straining against his huge hands.

"Who the fock are you, girlie-man?" he demanded. Then Vlad did something new. He let go of Nona and tossed Marcelin into the air and caught him like a rag doll. His tosses increased in altitude until the little man's head started grazing the ceiling. Some people began to titter, keeping their hands over their mouths, fearing that Vlad would think they were laughing at him, and he would start tossing *them* up into the air.

"Can't you do something about this?" Laurel implored, grabbing my arm.

"Like what?"

"I can't stand to watch it."

"Vlad isn't hurting him, just humiliating him," I said.

"Humiliating *is* hurting," she replied.

"Sean will hate him for a few days, especially since he thought Vlad was his friend. He gets babes for Vlad all the time."

"Babes," Laurel muttered, sneering.

"Well, that's what we call them. Sean is kind of like Pat. They are investment guys who hang out with rich people. Vlad is one of Sean's clients, and sometimes Vlad likes to humiliate people. After this, Sean will still say, 'The Bullies? Oh, yeah, they're my good friends. Especially Vlad Rybka.' The rest of us don't like Vlad or Sean, so why should we break this up?"

"Do you guys *really* dislike each other?"

"Most of the time, we do."

"Why?"

I shrugged. "Because we're all whores turning tricks for a pimp named Jacques."

Vlad tossed Sean Marcelin into the air once more, caught with him one arm and let him go. Marcelin grabbed Nona and hurried out the door.

"What's next?" Laurel asked. "Will someone call the cops?"

I shook my head. "Naw, that was just part of the evening's entertainment. Sean will be back for the next party, but Nona is history."

"Assholes!" Vlad yelled at the room. "Bunch of fockin' assholes! Take away Vlad's fun!" He stared at Laurel and me for a few moments, and I hurried over to Barrie.

"We gotta find the big guy something to do," I said. Barrie took hold of Vlad's arm and led him out to the swimming pool.

I went back over to Laurel and said, "Let's get together soon."

Paterson gave me the creeps, and I pondered for a moment why

Laurel dated him. All he had to offer her was big money.

I went outside to look for Weston, and suddenly felt a hand clamp down on my shoulder. At first I thought a bear had come down from the mountains to take me on. I was right, in a way.

"Hey, faggot, when did you become King Shit? Hey?" the bear asked.

"Vlad, lighten up, OK?"

"King Shit pussy asshole superstar faggot," Vlad said, squeezing harder.

"Let go, Vlad!" I screamed.

"Lighten up now, Vlad," Barrie said, appearing from nowhere. "Hear me? I repeat: 'Lighten up, Vlad.'"

Miraculously, Vlad did just that and went back inside to dress and sulk.

"Dammit!" I said as my shoulder, neck and head stung like bee's venom. "Son of a bitch! Motherfucker!"

Barrie produced a joint, lit it up and handed it to me. "The big guy doesn't like your attitude."

"He thinks I have an attitude? For real?"

"Yes," Barrie said. "He thinks you're disrespectful. He believes you turned us on to steroids and everyone could get into a shitload of trouble because of you. He's also convinced you're a closet homosexual."

"Well, maybe he's right." I tried to loosen up what the Russian had just grabbed. If Vlad had kept it up for a few more minutes, I would have ended up in the hospital. Vlad and Pavel, early on in my career, had pinned me face-down in the locker room and taped my buttocks together. When I pulled off the tape, hair and skin came off, too. Months passed before I could sit and shit comfortably.

I frowned. "If we win the Stanley Cup this year, Vlad should thank all of us juicers each time he admires his ring. We didn't get this far because of his fine defensive work. You, Ignas and I scored all the goals while Vladdy just stood on the ice and played with his dick."

"I'm just telling you what Vlad thinks," Barrie said.

"Vlad doesn't think, and that's his problem."

"Don't let him ever hear you say that. I won't always be around to save your ass after you piss him off." Barrie sneered. "Do you know what Paterson said to me? He wants to meet with me so he can make me a bunch of money with minimal risk and little effort."

"Then why don't you invest with him?"

"Because maybe he's full of shit. And even if he wasn't, I would have to meet with him and hang out with him. No fucking way."

"I like Paterson's girlfriend," I said.

"I like everyone's girlfriend," he said.

Barrie and I were friends because we admired each other professionally, and our friendship would continue for as long as we remained teammates. I felt proud to have Barrie as my friend and considered him one of the most resourceful and determined athletes I had ever encountered. A few years ago, an Edmonton Oilers defenseman hit him in the face with a hockey stick; Weston's teeth flew out of his mouth like Chiclets being shaken from a box. Barrie lay sprawled on the ice for a couple of minutes, then hurried into our trainer's room for some quick surgery to trim his dangling roots.

After sucking down a couple of gooey, high-protein canned drinks, he went back out to play. He stayed in for the rest of that game, and later seduced a couple of young women in a trendy bar.

"What are your ambitions?" he once asked me. "What is your direction in life?"

I shrugged. "I didn't know I needed ambition or direction. I'm too busy just being Chris Cross."

I knew other players, tedious people who studied the Toronto Stock Exchange and the Bayporte real estate market. They bought their wives BMW, sent them shopping at the Rolex and Brioni boutiques, or simply kept knocking them up. "The NHL? We'll be gone tomorrow, or the day after," they said to me. "We need to take advantage of our big paydays while we can."

Once Jacques released them, or they simply retired as a means of escaping the exhaustion and exasperation of the NHL, many would become complacent West Shore realtors or public relations consultants, playing games where nobody would give them concussions or knock out their teeth.

"Look at these people," Barrie said, pointing at the dancing, sweating, groping people at the party. "They seem to believe that all their wantonness is acceptable."

"Well, isn't it?" I asked.

"Decadent, depraved and dissolute." He stared at them with the wide-eyed fascination of a little boy checking out Siegfried and Roy's white tigers in Las Vegas.

"So they're just kicking back and having fun."

"Life," Barrie declared, "is one big hockey game. Power plays, slap shots, fights and penalties. It's all there."

"And we're a couple of superstars in that game, at least for now. I hope it goes into overtime."

He didn't answer me, he just stared into the swimming pool, as if the answers to life's deepest and most vexing questions swam about in the pool's blue depths.

"Sometimes I get confused, Cross. I think I know what I want and go after it, and I usually get it because I'm Barrie Weston, captain of the Bullies, and people are happy to give me what I ask for. But sometimes, once I get what I want, I start to think that maybe it's *not* what I want. Once I have it, it loses its value. It's a difficult thing to articulate…"

"The thing to remember," I said, with the self-importance of Socrates having discovered some essential truth, "is that life's a bitch and then you die."

Just then, some redheaded girl ran screaming out into the pool area as Vlad, clad only in his Jockey briefs, chased her. Around and around they went. Vlad and the girl laughed, then so did everybody else. He said, "You focking tease!" The girl jumped into the pool and everyone laughed some more.

"People love hockey because it's so much like life and often much better," Barrie said. "You shoot and score. You work together. If the other guy hits you, you hit back twice as hard. No politics, no brownnosing. How satisfying is that?"

Vlad watched the girl emerge from the pool, then he threw her back in. A couple of dozen partygoers stood watching and chuckling.

Vlad stuck both middle fingers at the pool and called it some names in Russian.

"Why do so many people envy us?" I asked Barrie. "We get paid to beat the shit out of each other."

Vlad threw the girl back into the water once more, and the spectators went back inside. Just then I saw a flash of light and heard tires squeal. Had someone been spying on us from the street?

"We're elite athletes who get out there and give the world a thrill the way Sinatra, Elvis and the Beatles did. That's the right way of looking at it, if not the accurate way," I told myself.

"Did you say something?" Weston asked.

"I'm just thinking out loud." I gestured to the girl as she pulled the hair out of her eyes and coughed up a bit of chlorinated water. "Is Vlad going to drown her or carry her off into the sunset?"

"What are you babbling about?"

"Just my usual babble."

The girl got out of the water, crept up behind Vlad and, her face contorted in rage, thumped him on the back. He spun around, grabbed her hair, backhanded her across the face, then tried to pull off her waterlogged jeans. She pried herself away and ran into the house.

"Well," Barrie said, "so much for Vlad meets girl. Cross, let's sit down." We settled into a couple of lounge chairs. "What's on your busy, troubled mind?"

"You really want to know? I'm freaking out about my meeting with Jacques tomorrow."

"Why? You've been playing great hockey. He should give you a raise."

"He's going to say, 'Cross, I've been hearing rumors that you are sticking a needle in your ass.'"

"Then you should say, 'Jacques, I'm the team's best supplier of anabolic steroids. If you get rid of me, you won't win any Stanley Cups.'"

"Shit." I chuckled. "That's not such a bad idea. I'll walk into his office tomorrow morning and say, 'Jacques, I believe that the intelligent, educated use of steroids and growth hormone will become so widely accepted in the years ahead that virtually everyone will be using it. Every hockey, football, baseball and basketball player will be using steroids and each sport as a result will be much more exciting and entertaining. It will extend beyond the playing field so that those in the stands, the fans, will be juicing, too. We'll all live longer and better.' No, that wouldn't fly with him."

Barrie grinned. "Especially since we've outplayed everyone this year and the media are saying, 'Why did those bums suddenly get so good? They must be doing something sneaky. Let's look at this very closely.'"

I nodded. We both stared into the endless, temporarily cloudless sky, and I wondered when the rain would come pissing down on us again. Donny Bourdin had a big house; he had overpaid for it and would probably have to sell it once his huge NHL paychecks stopped coming in. I wondered what I liked about Donny, and my ambivalence extended to Barrie. Weston, like most other sports stars, could be manipulative, exploitative and opportunistic. Once, he had confided to me, "I continue our friendship just to alienate all those people who dislike you. You spend so much time online trying to improve your mind, and you don't seem any smarter because of it."

Barrie, still looking up at the sky, said, "I have no fear."

"What?"

He shrugged. "I'm not afraid. I have no fear."

"Don't you? I thought we all did. Fear of losing, fear of failure, fear of Jacques. Fear was the thing that got me to start juicing. I knew that if I didn't start sticking a needle in my butt and give myself that extra edge, Jacques would have cut me loose. It was that same fear that made the rest of you guys start juicing, too."

"You sound like you're complaining," Barrie said. "You shouldn't complain. Things are pretty OK."

"They could be much better."

"They could be much worse. You need to savor the good for what it is, then value the bad as an opportunity to improve yourself." Weston kept looking up at the sky. I did likewise. We stayed silent for a long time.

I peered up at the stars but couldn't tell one from another, so I got bored with it. "I wonder why we do these things—play hockey, travel all the time, chase women. This crazy life."

"Well, if you quit doing it, fifteen minutes later you'd start to miss it."

Barrie had a point. I would miss my hockey life. I looked around and noticed that everyone had gone inside or left altogether in search of a new party.

I nodded off a couple of times in the lounge chair and finally got up. "Barrie?"

He said nothing.

I went back into the house. Debris lay scattered everywhere. Donny's state-of-the-art sound system kept playing some Britney Spears or Lady GaGa song about getting laid or being famous, and I wondered if I would ever get Laurel's phone number. I heard noises coming from the bedroom, so I went in to check it out.

Everyone shushed me as I opened the door.

Donny Bourdin stood naked at the foot of his bed, holding a stopwatch and thrusting his penis into the vagina of a young blonde on all fours. At the other end of her, Denis Pilon stood, his phallus sliding into and out of her mouth.

"What's with the stopwatch?" I asked.

"We're timing this. She wants to do adult videos," Donny replied.

"She has charisma," I said.

"She wants to do every player in the NHL," Donny explained as he pumped away. "She'll do you, too, if you want to wait till we're through."

For a moment, I nearly said yes. But then I thought of HIV, AIDS and herpes. "I'll tell Barrie to join you. He would enjoy this."

I headed down the hallway and I saw Weston stumbling around.

"What's goin' on?" he asked, running a hand through his messy hair.

"They're waiting for you in the bedroom. They got a kinky scene going on."

He brightened up. "Show me the way."

I pointed to the bedroom door.

"How come you're takin' off?" he asked.

"I got some porn movies downloaded at home and I want to jerk off for a few hours."

Barrie shrugged. "Whatever turns you on."

I nodded and went to get my car as Britney or GaGa kept singing.

2

I woke up at sunrise, full of anxiety over my upcoming meeting with Jacques. I tried to get back to sleep, but after some frustrating minutes of laying still with my eyes shut, I climbed out of bed and ambled over towards my bathroom. My father had always told me that lifelong health began with taking a dump in the morning; he probably would have warned me not to shoot steroids. I ran the shower nice and hot, letting the power jets pound my head, neck and shoulders. Now mostly awake, I toweled off and wondered about breakfast when my iPhone rang.

"Cross, it's me." Monique. "I wanted to catch up with you last night."

"Me, too. I ended up staying out late."

"Were you up this early?" she asked.

"I wanted to sleep in, but my brain and body had different ideas."

"Want to get together tonight?"

"Is your old man out of town today?" I asked.

"Yes. He's flying back here tomorrow."

"I'll call you after dinner tonight."

"Sounds good." Click.

My kitchen, like the rest of my home, remained filthy much of the time. I rarely tried to clean up after myself, and probably thought my messes would disappear on their own. Spilled coffee blackened my countertop; dirty dishes lay piled up in the sink. At least I had fresh, cold beer in my fridge. I kept my priorities straight.

I showered, shaved and got dressed for my meeting with Jacques. Appendy, my housekeeper, would be in this week. She had a key to my front door, so I locked it, got into my car and drove off to the Nu West Sports skyscraper, one of Bayporte's tallest, ugliest highrises. Jacques called me in once to demand an explanation for my decision to attend practice in a tuxedo.

Jimmie Gish, one of our coaches, raged at me during a training session because of my formal dress. "Crossley, if I was Jacques, I would trade your ass immediately!"

"If you were my boss, I would demand a trade!" I retorted.

I chuckled about my exchange with Gish as I looked up at the huge dark-glass building that had Nu West Sports scrawled at the top. In the building's parking lot, I eased into a space marked AUTHORIZED PARKING ONLY. I had no such authorization and cared very little. Nu West Sports had never ticketed nor towed anyone.

The big elevator doors swung open at the top floor, and I stepped out into a world of Bullies-themed, hand-drawn artwork. Last year, blown-up photos appeared everywhere on the walls, which I preferred to these new paintings and sketches of anonymous, scowling men in silver and black.

I loved hockey, but would it love me back if it knew about my juicing?

"I'm here to see Jacques," I told the receptionist.

She called his secretary. "Chris Crossley is here to see Coach. I assume he has an appointment."

I nodded that I *did* have an appointment and took a seat. The reception area of the front office seemed as fancy as a millionaire's home. I wanted to take off my shoes and socks and dig my toes into the thick shag carpeting. The air always smelled of perfume, too.

Norm Freelan, the team's business manager, turned the corner, his rayon shirt already badly pitted up. "Cross," he said, "what's the deal with your pizza bill in Phoenix? Five large pies?"

"We got hungry," I said.

"You had a per diem for food. That pizza order should have come out of your own pocket. Why did you try to bill the team for it?"

I shrugged. "It seemed like a good idea at the time."

"Don't let it happen again." He swallowed and wiped his brow. Confrontations really wore him out. "Why so much food?"

"A better question would be, 'Why not?'"

"Warren will shit when he sees that bill." Warren Gotch, the

Bullies' general manager and director of player personnel, threw a temper tantrum whenever he caught players trying to bill the team for things like pizzas, liquor and lap dances from strippers.

"Tell Warren that we needed some sustenance and enjoyed ourselves immensely," I said.

In truth, Barrie and I had cleaned out our Phoenix hotel room's minibar and invited some teammates to come in, play cards and listen to music. We passed the hash pipe and played our Doors downloads. We got the munchies and pigged out on pizzas. I didn't worry about it; Warren would just deduct the cost of the pies from my salary.

"Coach will see you now, Chris," the receptionist said.

I made my way past the offices of the Bullies' executive staff and finally reached Jacques' big corner of the Bullies' world. "Hey, Lynette," I said to his secretary.

"Sit over there," she ordered. "I'll buzz him and let him know you're here."

I sat and browsed at the copies of *Bullies Today* that fanned across a coffee table. "Beautiful," I said.

"Excuse me?" Lynette asked.

"This magazine has a photo of me in it. I feel like I'm famous or something."

"Well, isn't that special?"

Just then Jacques' door opened and out walked Warren, looking past me. "He's waiting for you."

Warren Gotch, a spectacularly revolting human being, had a face disfigured by acne scars and a disastrous haircut, as if he'd gone to his barber and said, "Make my head look like a cancerous growth." Tall but narrow-shouldered and potbellied, he wore polyester suits that only added to his ungainliness. Much of his job involved overseeing the scouting and acquisition of draft choices and free agents. Utterly lacking in ethics, integrity or honesty, Gotch became infamous for failing to fulfill his promises, and everyone dreaded his oily face and flaccid handshake. Behind his back, we called him Gotcha, as in, "Warren's 'gotcha' by the balls."

With degrees in accounting and business administration, Gotcha had few equals in negotiating contracts with players' agents, broadcast companies and apparel manufacturers. Currently the most successful general manager in the NHL, Warren had taught me that reading a contract could be far more challenging than reading an opponent's strategy. In the NHL, a shrewd negotiator made far more money than the finest forward.

Jacques sat at his desktop computer as I entered his office. He nodded for me to sit at his desk, and he kept typing and looking at his computer screen. A handsome man, tall and tanned, with a full head of graying hair, he wore a sweater saying BAYPORTE HOCKEY on the left breast.

I knew how much Jacques relied on his data about our team. His coaches assembled all the footage from our games and used that information to evaluate everyone's performance. A player's standing with the team came down to his numbers: playing time, goals and assists and so on. Jacques stared at the screen, his eyes astute and merciless.

Suddenly he turned from the computer and looked at me. "Well, Cross, how goes it?" he asked in the French accent so familiar to everyone who listened to the six-o'clock sports report.

"Excuse me?"

"Is life OK?"

I sat back and said, "When I play well, I feel well."

Jacques smiled. "Me, too. When *we* play well, *I* feel well. The reason I called you in here, Cross, is to discuss with you a very serious matter." He paused, his face quickly growing dark. "As I'm sure you know, the world of sports—not just hockey, but all sports, even at the non-professional level—has had to cope with the allegations of performance-enhancing drugs. Even the very top players in every game have been accused of using steroids. Recent studies have suggested that even high school athletes have begun using steroids to get bigger, stronger and faster, and that naturally is a very disturbing thing to me, and I'm sure it disturbs you as well.

"The media have reported widespread charges of steroid use among elite athletes, and these reports, unfortunately, have often generated more public interest than the sporting events themselves. The use of steroids, and the public's interest in the athletes who use them, will surely continue for some time. Mainly, this is because the overwhelming majority of today's and tomorrow's athletes have no reluctance to use steroids in order to improve their performance. Frankly, I believe that these very young athletes are taking steroids because the athletes have parents and coaches who want these youngsters to have that extra edge. Are you aware of what steroids are?"

"I've heard things." I relaxed, pleased by his presumption of my innocence or ignorance.

"Steroids." That word freaked him out. So did the words *death*, *cancer* and *bankruptcy*. "They are synthetic derivatives of testosterone, a naturally occurring male anabolic hormone. The anabolic effect is for the user to retain as much of his dietary protein as possible in order to grow bigger, stronger muscles.

"An athlete on steroids, of course, gets significantly more of this hormone in order to build bigger muscles and enhance physical performance. Athletes find that steroids will give them far more stamina and resiliency by acting as a buffer when lactic acid fills an athlete's muscles and tires him out. Athletes on steroids can run faster and farther as their endurance is doubled or tripled. Steroids, therefore, offer an athlete a major edge. Have you heard of 'stacking'?"

"No, sir," I lied. What juicer wouldn't know about stacking?

"Stacking is the practice of using more than one steroid at a time. Medical professionals agree that the stacking of steroids, when done under expert supervision, can make an extraordinary improvement in an athlete's performance without making himself look like a freak, if you will."

"I understand." I wondered when he would bring up drug testing.

"The NHL, of course, doesn't give each player a urine test; it's a 'no notice' test and you haven't had one yet, not that you would have had any difficulty passing it, no pun intended." He smiled. I smiled back. "I know, Cross, that you are a person of the highest integrity who would never do anything to compromise this team, and we have a player fail a drug test. Can I count on you to say no to steroids and report to me if you observe any steroids being used within the organization?"

"Absolutely, sir. I promise to do the right thing."

Our meeting ended soon afterwards. I drove over to our practice facility and pondered Jacques' words and my own future in the NHL. Steroids and drug testing. I had read an article online about a guy who coached athletes on beating drug tests; each athlete, by using only certain drugs at certain dosages, would stop just in time for his body to eliminate all traces of the drug and pass the test. I suspected, and certainly hoped, that the NHL and other top-level sports used the cheapest, most unreliable testing methods so that everybody passed.

Many of my teammates were already at the clubhouse when I arrived there, just after ten. They would play DVDs of recent games just before lunchtime. Inside, I stopped and looked at the notice I now knew by heart.

ALL MEMBERS OF OUR TEAM MUST BE FULLY DRESSED IN FRONT OF THE PUBLIC. HOCKEY FANS DON'T LIKE SLOBS.

WARREN GOTCH

I went into the locker room and opened the long, narrow metal box to which I had been assigned. Inside, I found scraps of fan mail, a few notes I had written to myself and one of my black leatherette injection kits. After changing into a jockstrap and T-shirt, I grabbed the kit, hurried into the men's washroom and locked myself inside a stall.

I opened the kit and withdrew a syringe, rubbing alcohol, a couple of cotton balls and a small bottle of Winstrol. After rubbing the intended target on my left buttock, I loaded the syringe with my current dose of juice and injected it with only momentary discomfort.

"Oh, Mrs. Crossley," I murmured, "would you look at what your son Chris is doing?"

Soon I entered the training room. This place always reminded me of a hospital's emergency room, where everyone in sight, bleeding or not, loudly and desperately demanded immediate attention.

"I need a rubdown," I told our trainer, Duncan McCallum.

He scowled. "Can't you see I'm busy?"

"OK." I sang along to the Alanis Morissette song on the sound system. Alanis belonged on my very long, and growing, list of Canadian Entertainers Who Permanently Emigrated After Becoming Successful in the States.

"You know, Cross, hockey attracts every kind of weirdo, but you—stop that bloody singing!—must be the most eccentric character I've encountered yet. Get up on the table."

About fifteen minutes later, I stripped and climbed into the whirlpool. At first, as always, I felt like a lobster being dropped into boiling water for someone's dinner. But soon the hot water soothed me and I closed my eyes.

"Hey, fellow!" exclaimed Roderick Rainey, who came by each day because apparently he had nothing better to do. Roderick owned the Bayporte Bullies. Years earlier, he'd paid a modest sum for this go-nowhere franchise, but now business analysts claimed he could sell it for a hundred million dollars or more. He spent more time here, among the players, than he did in his lavish office at the Nu West skyscraper. He told the media that the Bullies were part of his family. During training camp, his children shared living quarters with his players. Roderick lived there, too, and wandered about the place as if we were all one big clan—I thought of us as the Manson Family— and he freely dispensed advice to his children and players even on the most personal matters.

Each player tacitly received an invitation to join the family as soon as he had survived two seasons. Unacceptable Bullies quickly became Jets, Coyotes or Sharks. I considered myself the Raineys' reluctant relative and avoided Roderick's spoiled brats as they shouted and skateboarded up and down the hallways past sleeping players. The kids barged into the men's quarters and later giggled to each other about what they'd seen. I tried not to think about being employed— owned?—by an aging creep who liked ogling naked hockey players.

"Chris Cross!" Roderick said, approaching the whirlpool in his usual dark track suit and black runners. "How's it hangin'?"

"It's still there, Rod," I said.

"How do you like your skates?" he asked. "I've been meeting with the manufacturer, and they have some ideas about improving the fit, the blade, everything."

"We can always use a better skate," I told him.

"You've been playing great hockey, Cross. The kids and I can't stop talking about you."

"Good to know."

"I talked to Thornton the other day," he said. "I think he's finally ready to marry Monique. Good for him, eh?"

"I agree."

Thornton Rainey, a colossal fuckup, had flunked out of a half-dozen American colleges and been fired from every job he'd ever held. Roderick, Thornton's much older brother, chuckled at Thornton's countless blunders, the way a sibling can laugh when his whole family is set for ten lifetimes and can afford to indulge a loser. Thornton, ugly and dishonest, had gained admission into the Northup University School of Business Administration after Roderick called in some favors. As a graduation gift, Roderick named Thornton president of the Bayporte Bullies, a title of virtually no consequence.

"Thornton thinks you're a nice fellow," Roderick said as I boiled in the whirlpool. "The kids like you, too, so I want you to think seriously about becoming a more permanent member of our clan."

"Do you want to adopt me?"

Roderick threw back his head and laughed. "Oh, that's funny! Seriously, Cross, you should think about getting hitched again. Marriage is a good thing for a man. Monique has made Thornton much happier. I'm proud of him for going out into the world and finding such a fine woman. Have you met her?"

"Once or twice." Three nights a week, actually. A fine woman? Yes, she was that. In more ways than Roderick knew.

"She represents the stability that he needs. Now he can settle down and help me run this hockey team." Roderick leaned over towards me, licking his lips. "Not that the team really needs his help or mine, when we have guys like you on the ice to score the goals and thrill the crowd."

"I aim to please."

"You should think about remarrying," he repeated, staring at my nipples. I was afraid the little bastards would become erect and give him the wrong idea.

"I will do that, Rod. But for now, I'm giving divorce a chance."

He frowned. "Divorce is a difficult thing. Your ex is a Christian, right?" he asked.

"I guess."

"And you were married in church?"

"Yes, but I can't remember which one."

He shook his head. "It's sad that she wasn't the wife you wanted and needed." He returned his attention to my body. "You guys are all starting to look like a bunch of Arnold Schwarzeneggers. You're getting more buff and cut every day. Just a few years ago, you were as skinny as your hockey stick."

"Eating right and working out," I said. "That's the ticket."

"How is everything else? You holding up OK?"

"Yeah, I'm feeling pretty good."

"Glad to hear it. I should get out there and do my exercises, too."

He turned around and left.

I closed my eyes and sighed. Roderick skated with us, lifted weights and rode the stationary bicycle. Later, standing among the coaches, he watched us do our drills and discussed us with the coaches. He and his brother owned most of the team; Jacques and Gotcha owned the rest.

Rainey spent a few minutes each day consulting with Doctor Harri, our spiritual advisor, who traveled with us and gave us inspirational talks. Whenever we struggled, people said Doctor Harri and God failed to agree on the right hockey strategy for us.

I got out of the whirlpool and stared at the body Rainey had just admired, hoping he would never like it too much.

We sat down to review the videos of past games. The hum of the DVD player and Jacques' loud baritone made me uneasy. Playing hockey, difficult enough under the best of circumstances and against the weakest opponents, became torturous when we had to sit in plastic molded chairs in a dark room, watching our boneheaded moments on a big screen as our teammates groaned along with us. Jacques reversed and advanced the disk so rapidly that we all shook and jerked like epileptics on screen.

He always seemed to view each player's performance with an eye for its defects rather than strengths, because we were "paid great money to play great hockey." He also believed he had "an obligation to show everybody which players weren't playing their best."

"See this one?" Jacques froze the screen on the large figure of a lone player apparently staring off into space. "Synan, why were you on the other side of the rink from everyone else?"

John Synan, a defenseman, looked down and shook his head. "I don't know what to say."

"Say whatever is in your heart," Jacques retorted.

Everyone laughed. He ran the DVD some more. Our team had moved up the ice fast; we had them outnumbered five to four. Synan just stood there, oblivious to everything around him. Jacques returned to the frozen image of Synan spacing out. Most of us, sitting in the darkened room, tried to close our eyes or look away.

"Synan, I will ask you again: why were you on the wrong side of the rink for close to three minutes?"

"I really don't know, sir," Synan answered, his voice barely audible.

"You don't know," Jacques said. "We have no use for players who don't know what they're doing out on the ice. No use at all."

No use at all. You're fucked, man.

Jacques fast-forwarded past my third-period goal, although a few players glanced at me and gave me a discreet thumbs up. I smiled at them and thought about what I'd like for lunch, when Jacques barked out the two syllables that meant trouble.

"Crossley!"

A bad moment. We had the puck deeply in the other team's zone and I needed to stay out of Weston and Bourdin's way so they could take turns making shots on goal. I ended up in the crease, right in front of the goalie; an opposing player got behind me and hooked me between the legs with his stick, so I couldn't move. He used me as a human shield against Bourdin's slap shot. I sat in that dark, lonely room and closed my eyes as the whole team roared at my expense.

"Not funny," Jacques said. "Such sloppiness can cost a team the Stanley Cup. If you can do without winning the Cup, go ahead and laugh. I will be here long after you've gone off to sell cars or real estate."

He reran the footage several more times. We started to look like a bunch of Ice Capades performers.

Finally, Jacques ended the footage and turned on the lights.

"Next thing is for everyone to do an hour of weight training, then some ice time. Synan, you wait here. I need to speak to you."

We all got up and filed out of the room. Synan sat there, knowing he would not be winning a Stanley Cup with the Bayporte Bullies or anyone else.

When we got to the locker room, we saw the equipment manager emptying Synan's locker. We all shrugged at each other, as if to ask, 'We knew *he* would be cut, but who's next?' The next time we saw Synan, he would be in another uniform. Or we would never see him again.

"One hour! Starting now!" Jimmie Gish hollered.

We all grunted, strained and sweated through exercises with exotic-sounding names: cable-shot rotation, wall stride, Swiss-ball rollout, cross-lateral reverse lunge, Swiss-ball posterior bridge. Our muscles bulged and our limbs became as striated as an artist's sketch. Barrie and I, naturally, had juiced up before this session and felt as if we could work out all day without becoming fatigued.

'Try to relax,' I had muttered to him during one of our early injection sessions in the men's washroom stall. He made little noises as the needle penetrated his flesh.

'If anyone overhears us,' he muttered back, 'we'll have some explaining to do.'

'If anyone asks, we'll just tell them we were in this stall bumholing each other.'

Barrie stifled a chuckle as I completed the injection.

'I think I can inject you,' he said.

'Give it a try.'

We traded places and he shot me up with ease.

"Barrie and Cross! That's what I like to see!" Jacques hollered with a smile as we completed a particularly grueling exercise. Later, on the ice, we did drills that emphasized skating agility and stick handling. Jacques divided us up into teams for the informal practice games that I loved so much because they reminded me of those pickup floor hockey matches during my childhood. As kids, we usually ended up beating the shit out of each other, but that was half the fun of it. Today, with the Bullies, Ignas, Weston and I took on Bourdin, Pilon and Horton in a short, enjoyable game intended just to keep us loose. My butterflies started up a bit as I took my spot on a power play and waited for the moment that Weston, getting the puck from Ignas, would pass it to me, as I tried not to think about Jacques scrutinizing me as I anticipated the puck.

After the practice game, I felt rejuvenated and refreshed. Barrie and I joined some of our teammates in the sauna. Within minutes, I felt sheets of sweat sliding down my body and my lungs ached from the heat.

"I've been thinking," said Vlad. He often sat and pondered, then shared his insights as if he were the first person ever to make such mental breakthroughs. "We get paid too much. We should get just minimum wage, plus extra if we do something good, like score a goal or punch out someone who deserves it." As an "enforcer," he protected Barrie Weston, Mark Ignas and me.

"Vlad," said Wally Horton, "you are full of shit."

"We should work on commission," said Vlad. "Get money for each goal, more money for each head injury inflicted on opponent."

"Vlad, just shut up, OK?" Horton rolled his eyes.

We all stayed silent. Presently, I went to take a shower, then got dressed and left the building. I got back into my car and searched for the right satellite station to play.

I drove east, with the music blaring, windows rolled up and air conditioning shooting frigid air into my happy face. Breezing through downtown Bayporte, feeling good because of having satellite radio and a good job, I looked at the other drivers and saw sad faces, clenched teeth and unknotted ties. They all reminded me of Travis

Bickle from *Taxi Driver*, and I asked myself, 'Which one will snap first and go on a shooting spree like Travis did?'

I headed downtown for a drink at the Imperial Club. On the 30th floor of the Nu West skyscraper, the Club, a vision of staid opulence, featured floor-to-ceiling windows, gleaming hardwood floors and fine leather furniture. Arguably the fanciest drinking place in western Canada, the Club had black-tied staff who served cocktails to those fortunate enough not to be the low-wage administrative flunkies and customer-service slaves who fueled the Bayporte economy.

I rode up to the Club with dark-suited men who pretended they did not recognize me.

We all floated into the seductive darkness of my favorite place in which to drink for free.

"May I help you?" asked the bartender.

"I'll have a beer," I said.

"Canadian?"

"No, Blue." I wanted a Budweiser or Miller, but Roderick Rainey, who owned the Club, insisted that they serve only domestic brands. Fortunately, my drinks went on his tab.

I gazed out the huge windows. Bayporte, the city with everything: mountains to the north, the mighty Tyson River to the south, and a clutch of glittering skyscrapers. On such a sunny day, the photographers would be out taking pictures to fool the rest of the world into believing that this Canadian city always looked so wonderful. Bayporte on a rainy day could be as coyote ugly as any place I had ever visited.

Near a window, some men stood talking loudly and laughing, gesticulating, even shaking their fists at each other.

"I'll tell you what I told my kid," said one of them, a man with a goatee. "I said, 'If I ever catch you selling, buying or using crack or meth, I'll turn you over to the cops, and I don't mean maybe.'" He added, "Phil Burnell had the right idea."

Phil Burnell, a prominent Bayporte entrepreneur, had caught his mostly naked, underage daughter getting high with her boyfriend. Burnell sent her to a psychiatric hospital in the States, where they filled her with medication and gave her daily talk therapy to help her understand her misdeeds. Burnell told a Bayporte news service that his daughter, now back home, had become "very cooperative."

"Chris Cross!"

I looked behind me, to see who had spoken my name. My face fell.

Steve Yon. I liked to call him Steve Yawn. A rich lawyer, he and I had met at some social functions. "Come over and say hi," he said now, leading me over to his little group, which included the man with the goatee I'd just overheard. Yawn quickly introduced me to his companions as they resumed their conversation.

"Drugs are drugs," explained the man with the goatee. "Some drugs definitely enhance athletic performance. Jose Canseco, after he retired from baseball, wrote a book bragging about all the steroids he'd shot in his ass."

"And what about Barry Bonds?" asked a man named Bob, whose face bore the scars of alcoholic desolation. "It's pretty obvious that he was using steroids because he got so big."

"Or Lyle Alzado," I said. "He overdid it and ended up with a brain tumor."

"Lyle who?" asked Bob.

"Exactly," I said.

During my marriage, Steve Yawn invited my wife and me to his home one evening. I had smoked some pot beforehand, so my wife insisted on driving. She parked our car near the Bentleys and Rolls Royces surrounding Yawn's magnificent West Shore home. Steve met us at the door, fixed us cocktails and introduced us to everyone else. Then he played O Canada on the piano and asked us to sing along. He had invited us to a secret-society meeting of some kind.

A couple of hours later, they gave us little slips of paper and told us to write the names of people we thought might be terrorists or druggies. I couldn't think of anyone, so I wrote the name Roderick Rainey.

"Steroids, Cross," said Bob, the drunk at the Club. "Do you approve of that shit?"

"I think," I replied, "that I want another beer."

"Seriously, Cross, what do you think about drug-testing and suspensions? Steroids can't be as popular as I've heard," Bob persisted.

Just then my second beer arrived. The guy with the goatee said, "With the brutal competition in sports, I guess those players are looking for any kind of advantage they can get."

"I'll drink to that." I tipped my bottle in his direction.

"Let's talk about hockey," said Bob. "How have you guys managed to beat New York, Boston, Pittsburgh? That Sidney Crosby is one bloody tough son of a bitch."

I shrugged. "They're all tough, even the ones who don't look tough. But the fans don't want to hear that. They don't want to hear any excuses, they just want to see their team win games."

"Remember the game when you and Ovechkin punched it out?" the goateed guy asked. "I thought you were going to kill each other."

"You mean we didn't?"

They threw back their heads and howled.

I laughed, too. I laughed at these hotshot businessmen, responsible for billions of dollars of investors' money and the livelihoods of thousands of people, falling over each other at the wisecracks of a hockey player. Maybe, I guessed, these high-powered men in suits were really just boys who still wanted to become jocks when they grew up.

"You really got banged up last year," Steve Yawn said.

"I banged up some other folks, too."

Everyone chortled.

"Which of your injuries was the worst?"

"Probably my bruised testicle."

Gales of laughter over my bruised testicle? Shame on them.

"A bruised testicle was the worst injury? Really?"

"Well, have *you* ever had a bruised testicle?" I asked. "The poor little bugger was on the disabled list for a month. I had to put a little silk pillow underneath him when I played."

"I've never had a bruised testicle," he said.

"Want one now?"

The guy grabbed his stuff and they all doubled over in merriment. Good for me, breaking the chops of Bayporte's business elite.

"Aside from the testicle," the goateed guy asked, "which was your worst injury?"

"There is no second to a bruised testicle," I said. "Seriously, I got a knee in the back, and that really hurt."

"Yeah." The goateed guy nodded. "Back injuries really disable you. Can't walk, sleep, fuck..."

"Fucking is pretty difficult with a bruised testicle, too," I said.

"Who was the best player, ever?" asked Bob.

I'd heard this question too many times. I couldn't call one player better than another, especially when they played for different teams during different times.

"I've always thought Gretzky had the biggest impact," I said.

"I would say Bobby Orr," Steve Yawn said. "He didn't take crap from anybody. That's the trouble with Canada today. We're wimps."

"This wimp wants another beer," I said. I went over to the bar.

"Canadian?" the bartender asked.

"No." I thought for a moment. "A Dief." Diefenbaker, the smoothest, richest and most expensive brand in Canada, could be difficult to find.

"Don't have it."

"No Dief at the Club? For real?"

He just shrugged. "Canadian? Blue? Black Label?"

I nodded. "Canadian."

"How do you like my suit?" Steve Yawn asked his little group. He opened his jacket so we could see the designer label inside. "It's a Brioni knockoff that I got in Hong Kong. You can't tell it's not the real thing."

"How many times have you sent it to the cleaners?" the goateed guy asked.

"Never. I just bought it."

The goateed guy smirked. "It's a Kleenex suit. Send it to the cleaners once and it'll look like you've blown your nose into it."

Everyone laughed some more.

"I saw Roderick golfing on the weekend," the goateed guy said. Roderick Rainey played at West Shore's golf course, and they considered him their most valuable member. Roderick played poorly and cheated often. He also liked to play with people who didn't care how many strokes he shaved off his card. "He said he may be needing another body to complete a foursome, and he'll call me." The goateed man beamed.

I nodded, to show that I envied anyone fortunate enough to watch Roderick cheat, then I excused myself to use the washroom. The Club's toilets and urinals were made of the finest porcelain available; its doors were heavy, polished wood and its fixtures were golden and gleaming. Why did anyone need such a luxurious place in which to drop a deuce?

I locked myself inside a stall and sat on the throne. Gazing at the door, I found a small message etched into the heavy, dark wood. I looked closer, squinted, and read it:

RODERICK RAINEY BUGGERS LITTLE BOYS

The sky darkened fast as I headed to Monique's apartment. I turned off the radio after listening to the news for a couple of minutes. Each newscast seemed to be about death and brutality in town: in an all-night restaurant, a bunch of Asian gangsters and their women were having a meal at four in the morning when a bunch of rivals walked in, shot them all dead and walked out. The police called it one more battle in a very long war over crack and heroin profits. Bayporte, the cops conceded, had gangs, but so did all other major cities, and wars happened.

Driving away, I saw the Nu West Sports skyscraper in my rearview mirror. Sections of the building remained all lighted up. Jacques and his cronies sat up there, scrutinizing the footage from recent games and making plans for future changes.

Gotcha worked late, too; I could see his office lights on. As general manager, he worked endless hours, or maybe he just wanted to look super-busy to Roderick. I had a very memorable meeting once with Warren in his immaculate office, its walls decorated with hockey paraphernalia. Gotcha, talking on the phone as his secretary brought me in, just pointed at a seat and mouthed, *Sit.*

Warren always fidgeted as he sat; he swiveled from left to right in his chair. He guzzled coffee and couldn't keep still once his caffeine fix kicked in. He talked fast and interrupted people often. He hung up suddenly and offered me no smile or word of welcome.

My agent had already negotiated my contract. Gotcha said he wanted to see me only to dot the i's and cross the t's.

'So, Chris.' Warren had his iPad in front of him. He tapped on it and looked up at me. The guy who casually picked the pockets of broadcast networks and sports-apparel behemoths now had some business with me. 'I want to talk numbers with you.'

I squirmed. 'I thought you and my agent worked that out.'

'Different kind of numbers for this meeting. I have been looking at your statistics from the past couple of years or so: games, goals, assists, penalties, total minutes played.' He rattled off a series of numbers that were low and bad, then some that were good and high. I smiled at the good ones and frowned at the bad ones. 'Lately, your productivity has rivaled that of Crosby, Ovechkin and the Sedins.'

'I guess that's why you pay me the big bucks.' I smirked.

'Don't be a smartass. You were drafted by us as a player with the potential to be slightly better than average. You're not supposed to be a Sidney Crosby or Alex Ovechkin. You're not even a Barrie Weston or Mark Ignas, so I have to ask myself, "Why has Chris Crossley improved so much so suddenly?"'

'And the answer is?' I asked.

He gave me a condescending little smile. 'Oh, I think we both know the answer.'

'Can you give me a teensy little hint?'

He showed me his forefinger and pointed it upwards, as if it were a needle, and stuck it into his fanny.

I swallowed hard and did my best to look appalled. 'Are you

accusing me of using performance-enhancing drugs?'

'I'm not accusing anyone of anything, yet. I'm just trying to understand how, in the past months, you've tripled your endurance, nearly doubled your skating speed, and don't get me started on your strength of body weight. You've also grown two jersey sizes. So I ask myself again: "What's the deal with Chris Crossley?"'

'What's the deal with Ovechkin, Crosby and those other guys? Do you think *they* have been using performance-enhancing drugs?'

Gotcha shrugged. 'They don't play for the Bayporte Bullies, so they're not my problem.'

'What about Weston, Ignas and—'

'Leave them out of it. This is about you, not them. In fact, this conversation is completely confidential. Not even Jacques or Roderick should know about it, although I'm surprised they haven't spoken to you yet about this matter.'

I frowned. 'Warren, why are *we* having this conversation?'

He glowered at me. 'Because the Bullies are the biggest worst-to-first story in recent NHL history and everyone's talking about us. Personally, I'm wondering if I have a bunch of juicers on my hands. If I'm right, and there's a scandal, my method of damage control will be to blame you for all of it. You better hope you don't have to take a piss test anytime soon, guy.'

As I got nearer to Monique's apartment, I resolved not to think about that meeting with Gotcha again. For me. worrying about things always accomplished zero. By the time I reached Monique's front door, I felt cranky and unappreciated, in need of succor.

"I can get ready later," Monique said as I entered her apartment. "Want a quickie?"

"Naw. Anything good on Netflix?" I strode into her bedroom.

"Be gentle with me," I said as I climbed into bed. "Promise me you'll be gentle?"

"I promise," she replied. "I'll even respect you afterwards."

"Did I tell you?" she asked as we cuddled afterwards late at night.

"I got engaged."

"Congratulations, I guess."

"We're going for the ring next week at Boccasio's."

"Sounds expensive." Monique had been running around with Thornton for at least a couple of years. Her willingness to cheat on him indicated that she didn't want to marry him, but when your millionaire lover pops the question, you say yes.

Monique had moved to Bayporte from some village in Quebec, where she studied liberal arts at the local community college until, out of boredom, she became a Canadian Airways flight attendant. Her marriage to Thornton would change things between us, but for now, she had her own life apart from him; he paid all of her living expenses and she pocketed all of her airline paychecks.

"Should I be happy for you?" I asked her. "Have you set a date?"

She tossed back her hair. "Oh, we'll do it whenever. No hurry there. He even suggested that I keep this place to live in until we get around to tying the knot."

"He's either very understanding or completely stupid," I said.

We shared a joint. She got her drugs from Thornton, and he got his from wherever rich people got theirs. He gave her premium dope, so we smoked one long, fat joint and rolled another. Within minutes I held a bomber as long and thick as my finger. We passed it back and forth.

Her apartment had a spectacular view of downtown Bayporte and the mountains in the north. Dozens of apartment buildings in her neighborhood sat packed together, all with big price tags. I looked up and saw the running message at the top of the Nu West Sports skyscraper. This night, as usual, the message said GO BULLIES. Our team, always a special part of this city, inspired everyone to second-guess Jacques LaPierre and Warren Gotch about how to win a Stanley Cup.

I chuckled at the big gold message way up there in the sky, crawling along the top of the building like a stock-market ticker.

"What's funny?" Monique asked.

"The Nu West message."

"'Go Bullies.' So what? That's the team's nickname, right?"

"Yeah, *we* know that. But what if someone came to town who *didn't* know it? What would they think?"

"You tell me."

"In schools," I said, "they're really into this awareness thing about bullying. People wear pink T-shirts to promote the prevention of abusive behavior. Entire Websites deal exclusively with how to deal with mean kids. Roderick Rainey personally sponsors 'Let's Take Back Our Schools from the Troublemakers' campaigns."

She nodded. "All the while he has 'Go Bullies' on the top of his building. Maybe he should add the messages, 'Power to Punks' or 'Yea Sadists.'"

Monique got up and sauntered over to her sound system. Presently some insipid music from the 1970s came on. She loved music from that far in the past. Getting back into bed, she stared for a few moments at my flaccid penis. "What's wrong with your little thing? Has he gone to sleep?"

"Good dope makes him mellow."

"So, what's happening with Jacques?" I appreciated Monique's sincere concern for my welfare. She genuinely took an interest in me personally, not just sexually. I didn't have many people I considered my friends.

"Jacques says I'm to keep an eye out for steroids and report back to him about who's juicing."

"Sounds like he and Warren are getting pretty suspicious."

"Yes, ma'am. Of course, if we played without the steroids, we'd still suck. Roderick and the others want a Stanley Cup, but they don't want us using performance-enhancing drugs." I blew out some pot smoke. "Well, guys, sorry to tell you this, but you can't have it both ways."

"They also think that you're the one who started this whole doping thing with the Bullies, and they're right."

"Whose side are you on?" I asked her.

"Yours, of course." She kissed the tip of my nose.

I gave a short, bitter laugh. "Shit, I can't go fifteen minutes without talking, thinking or hearing about fucking steroids."

"Then let's change the subject. Wanna fuck some more?"

"Well, OK, if you insist."

3

"If no one else has said it to you yet, good morning!" Monique's clock radio had just turned itself on. Bryant Forrester, Bayporte's legendary air personality, did his usual *shtick*.

"Fuck you very much, Bryant," I muttered as I turned him off. I had met Forrester several times over the years. A rabid Bullies fan, he pumped my hand and beamed at me with such intensity that I feared he might kiss me. Forrester and his wife Frannie had entered Ed Lee's Chinese restaurant while Mark Ignas and I were on a double date. Forrester spotted us, came over and invited himself and Frannie to sit with us.

Frannie Forrester, from the Prairies, said to Ignas, 'Wow! I can't believe I'm sitting down to eat with one of *you* people!'

I sighed and drank more wine. Then I ordered another bottle and looked over at Ignas. He just rolled his eyes at me.

Frannie leaned in his direction and said, 'I have nothing against you Native people.'

'Frannie,' said Ignas' date, a blonde model, 'I don't like breaking bread with his kind. But I *do* love riding their nice big dicks.'

Frannie turned blue, about to vomit, and Bryant hustled her out of the restaurant.

"Ride *my* dick, Bryant," I muttered as I got out of bed and went to the bathroom to fill the tub and soak.

Monique wandered in with her iPad. She loved shiny gadgets. "There's something about you in here," she said. "They say you're the NHL's 'laff riot.'"

"I hope there's room in the Hall of Fame for funny guys like me. I really a special gift, you know. Humor is underrated and requires no needles or pills."

She handed me her iPad and I read the article. I felt so pleased at finding my name in print, and got enraged when they got my name or quotes wrong. Sports reporters were such douche bags. Often they didn't know jackshit about sports but pretended that they were experts on things quite beyond their comprehension. They covered sports because they didn't know how to do anything else.

The top stories interested me much more. Uncle Sam had finally pulled out of Iraq, but now Iran and Israel were snarling at each other. The poor Greeks' debt crisis exasperated the rich Germans. The world's financial crisis worsened. I handed Monique her iPad and closed my eyes. "It's all too fucked up for me."

She nodded and sipped at her gourmet coffee. "Remember the cops who Tasered that guy to death at the airport in Vancouver? That whole thing is still going on. They're talking about pressing charges against those cops after all. How long has *that* bullshit been going on?"

"Yeah, I remember. The dead guy's mother sued the cops for a million bucks or so. Must be fun being a cop, eh? Almost as much fun as being a hockey player." After a while I sighed and got up out of the tub, sloshing water around.

"Watch it!" Monique backed away. "You're getting me all wet!"

"Oops!"

"You could do with a shave and a haircut," she said.

"Yeah, I'll put that on my to-do list."

"Sad little soldier." She reached down and tugged on my reddened, shriveled member. "What do *you* want for breakfast, little soldier?"

"I'll just dunk him in some coffee and he'll be fine," I said. "Get me an Egg McMuffin."

"Get it yourself. Get me one, too."

"Never mind. What do you usually have for breakfast?"

"A chocolate doughnut."

"I'll have half of yours," I said.

"I take such good care of you!" She threw back her head and laughed. Then she left the bathroom.

I grinned in spite of myself. Monique, one of the most charming women I had ever met, had made a commitment to Thornton Rainey, a most undeserving man. As much as I wanted to spend the day laying naked in Thornton's fiancée's arms, I had things to do and places to go. I needed to get dressed, go home and put on some heavier clothing. A shower and shave wouldn't be such a bad idea, either.

I shivered at the cold, blustery morning as I climbed into my car. If I worked in an office, I would call in sick. Driving home, I listened to Bryant Forrester's bullshit for a few minutes, then turned him off and turned on satellite radio. I caught Richard Pryor halfway through *his* bullshit. I loved Pryor and had seen most of his movies, even the bad ones.

I drove faster in my desire to get home, then had to slow down when the traffic thickened. In Bayporte, too many people had cars but couldn't drive. Drivers here rammed into each other many times a day, squeezing BMWs and Volvos into accordions and sending broken, bloodied people to nearby emergency rooms.

The moment I arrived home, I knew I had trouble: I found my front door wide open. The maid, the wind, burglars? I tiptoed through my ransacked house. Someone had turned over my sofas and chairs and emptied my drawers. They could have broken or stolen most of what I owned, and I would have accepted such a loss with a shrug, because I had acquired much of my stuff at low cost, or no cost, from Bullies fans who worked in retail or wholesale. I refused to cry over any of it. The intruder had trashed my bedroom, too, but apparently departed without taking any of my property.

I hated being violated, of course, just as I dreaded the prospect of the bill from the cleaning service after the maids had tidied up my disaster area. I did not call the cops, because they would take reports and do nothing else for me. I tiptoed around some more and headed for my closet to get my parka. I put it on, went back into the living room and surprised my maid, Appendy.

"Eeeeek!" She clutched her chest and her eyes bugged out. Her cocoa-colored face momentarily turned several shades lighter.

"Appendy, don't scream in the morning," I said. "It makes me feel bad."

"Mister Chris, what has happened to your home? I am here to do my job and what am I seeing?" she said in her Indian accent. "I am coming in and saying to myself, 'Appendy, what is happening here?'"

"Burglary," I said.

"Hey?"

"Burglary. Break-in. Bad men come in and bust up all my shit."

"Oh, I am understanding you now." She started whimpering. "Poor, poor Ozzie."

"What happened to him?"

"Ozzie pass away."

Ozzie was my parrot, a gift from the owner of a pet store. I called him Ozzie because he screamed like the rock star Ozzie Osborne. He looked like the singer, too: gray and small-eyed.

"Ozzie's dead?" I had assumed the bird would outlive me. One time, after a luckless road trip, I had come home, crabby and forlorn, and thrown hockey pucks at my bird. I nearly hit Ozzie twice, and he flew onto my roof, making growling noises. I threw a few more pucks at him but missed.

My bird flew off, presumably forever, but returned a few days later, looking healthier than ever. I opened the door, and he walked in.

'Hey, motherfucker,' he said. Ozzie had a potty-mouth.

"Appendy, how did he die?"

"He just toppled over. The reverend say he probably died of heartbreak."

"Heartbreak, eh? Maybe the burglar scared him to death," I said.

"So we bury him already, Mister Cross."

I didn't ask where. I said a brief, silent prayer for the soul of a parrot named Ozzie.

"Appendy," I said, pointing at her boom box, "why are you carrying that thing?"

"I am having something to share with you, Mister Cross. My sister and I sang a song and we are wanting you to hear this. The reverend recorded it."

The reverend, a man with a beard and turban, sat in a huge Mercedes, waiting for Appendy. Apparently my maid had greater aspirations in life than cleaning houses. A devoted participant in Bayporte's large and influential Sikh community, she often worshiped at their gigantic nearby temple and seemed somehow related to every one of the myriad Indians in Bayporte. She regularly got time off from her job because of temple events or deaths in the family. She politely but relentlessly asked me for pictures of myself and other Bullies. A competent forger, she scribbled our names on the pictures and sold them to other Sikhs.

"Mister Cross," she said now, "you must be sitting down to enjoy this music."

"Appendy, we can do this another time. I have things to do today."

"I will not be taking very long. As soon as we are done with this I will be very busy making your home nice again." She'd never actually made my home nice once.

I sighed. "All right, but just a few minutes."

She smiled. "Very good. Then I will be very busy cleaning up after you."

I righted the sofa and sat down. I could picture the minister in the car outside, a big, impatient man tapping his fingers on the steering wheel while wondering if his girl Appendy would become an Indo-

Canadian Mariah Carey.

"Here is the song I have sent to Bryant Forrester," she said.

I nodded and sighed, knowing that her tape would go from Forrester's secretary directly into their circular file, where all the unsolicited music went. Appendy pressed the PLAY button on her discount-store boom box and the song sounded like hip hop meets gospel. I just stared at the boom box so I didn't have to look at Appendy.

"Christopher Crossley

Christopher Crossley

You make me feel so good..."

I groaned. "What the fuck, Appendy? You can't do that. You can't sing about *me* and send it out to Bryant Forrester—"

She frowned a bit, then smiled. "I have already sent it to him. He is your good friend. Are you thinking he will play my song and make it

'Number One with a bullet'?"

"I must leave now. Please clean up my mess. I will pay you time and a half." Barrie Weston said that Appendy, aside from being the worst maid in Canada, probably didn't even have a permanent-resident card. "Thank you for your concern about Ozzie."

I left my home and started for my car.

"I will be staying and working until your home is tidy again," she called out.

"Good day to you, sir," I said to the Sikh reverend as I passed by him. He smiled.

Rain started to fall, fat droplets from big black clouds. I drove slowly, turned up the volume on my satellite radio and got depressed about Ozzie. I hated myself for losing my temper and trying to puck him to death, and felt grateful that he loved me anyway. I'd wanted him to fly away for his own good, to join his brothers and sisters in the lush Canadian wilderness and make little Ozzies instead of mooching off a cynical hockey player in a heartless big city.

I admonished myself to quit worrying about my dead parrot and start worrying about who had broken into my home. Break-ins happened even in the best neighborhoods, and mine qualified as good but not great. Our most infamous street gangs, the Native Sons and World Brotherhood, had invaded houses near mine. I felt fortunate nobody had barged in one me, held me at gunpoint and sodomized me.

Flashing lights appeared up ahead. The rain had slackened up but the road remained slick and traffic each way scarcely moved. Royal Canadian Mounted Police cars and officers appeared. A semi had overturned, and its driver stood talking to the police, doubtless thankful that he and his load hadn't been scattered all over the roadway. Once I got past the accident scene, I sped up, trying to get to practice as fast as I could.

"We have many things we need to go through today. Gish will explain some things right now." Jacques said, wiping a trickle of sweat from his cheek.

"All right, I need your attention." Jimmie Gish hurried to the front of the room. "I want to see improvements immediately." He started to write something on the white board, but his felt pen had dried up. He capped it, threw it aside and looked for another one. He couldn't find one, and some of us began smirking.

"Shit," he muttered. "Anyway, in the past couple of weeks, we have spent far too many minutes in the penalty box, and while our opponents have outnumbered us on the ice—in other words, they were on power plays—they have scored more often than not." He rattled off a series of trivial statistics, ignoring the fact that we had won those games anyway. "We can't win a Stanley Cup from the penalty box."

Gish, a Bullies enforcer years earlier, coveted Jacques' job as an ideal way of continuing his NHL career. He had joined us as a skating coach and failed abysmally at every aspect of his job. Jacques kept Gish around because Roderick Rainey believed that Gish represented a useful and inspirational link to our team's past. Jacques, uncertain of what else to do with him, made Gish a sort of "coach at large," meaning that Gish did fun things like give us pep talks and teach us to provoke our opponents into fights so that they, not we, would do time in the penalty box. After a hellish losing streak last season, Jacques confidentially consulted us on the reasons for our sudden, despairing struggle. Nearly everyone blamed Jimmie Gish.

"I've broken it down," Gish explained, red-faced and shaking, as if he, too, were about to break down. "How many minutes does each player get on the ice? If he has a penalty, how long is each penalty? When we have all five men on the ice, how long do we retain possession of the puck? How many minutes do we spend on power plays, and how often do we score on power plays? If we give them advantages, they'll eat us for breakfast." He pounded on the podium for emphasis, and his audience sat up straight.

"Pay attention!" Gish demanded. Players sighed and grinned, looking away. Jimmie cleared his throat and shrugged. "I've done my best, Jacques. They're all yours. I guess they just don't want to win a Stanley Cup." He walked out of the room.

"You men need to have a professional attitude about all this," Jacques said, sauntering to the front of the room. "I have something here I want you to read. In fact, we will read it together."

He passed out sheets of paper to us. Soon we all had reading material, mostly a bunch of bullshit Gipper things he had copied from Hallmark cards. Most of the other players tapped their fingers or stared out into space.

"I hope you gentlemen respect the profundity of these words," Jacques said.

Behind me, Donny Bourdin sat snuffling and whimpering. "This is beautiful."

Barrie whispered, "I didn't know Bourdin could read."

"You are the elite," Jacques said. "The best of the best. We're here to make you better."

"Then get us some steroids," Barrie muttered, and I had to fight to keep from laughing.

"Do you have a problem, Crossley?" Jacques asked.

"No problem here, sir."

"You need to pay attention today. You are the person who has the most to gain by improving your attitude."

"Yessir." I kept my eyes glued to the handouts for the rest of the meeting. I could feel everyone's eyes on me, but I didn't look up or around.

Afterwards, we all boarded a bus bound for a community center's ice rink to practice. Fat raindrops pounded the bus as it crept through crowded city streets. By and by we reached our destination. We laced up our skates and got out on the ice. During these informal sessions, we usually divided into two groups of five quickly and commenced what amounted to pick-up games. I made sure I played alongside Barrie Weston and Mark Ignas. In the thrill of moving the puck down the ice with them, I became oblivious to my surroundings and collided with another player. I ended flat on my back and could hear the *thwack!* of my helmet striking the concrete-hard ice. Without the reinforced plastic headgear, I would have suffered a severe concussion. Even with the helmet, I got a bad headache but got back up without assistance.

"Son of a bitch," I muttered.

"Crossley, that's what happens when you daydream," Jacques shouted from the stands. I looked in his direction and nodded with a wave. He laughed and said something to Jimmie Gish.

We played on, and soon Weston, Ignas and I had a tidy little power play against the other squad. After we passed the puck back and forth a few times, I flipped it past Mike Fillo, who took every shot on goal as an affront to his manhood.

"Chris!" Jacques shouted right after my goal. "You see what staying alert will do for you?" He smiled and gave me thumbs up.

I nodded thanks and sat on the bench for the remainder of practice. Working out in an unfamiliar facility like this one disoriented me and I couldn't wait for our session to end. Back at the clubhouse, I felt cold and wanted to warm up in the whirlpool. In the locker room, I noticed Pavel slipping some live cockroaches into the jersey of Wally Horton, a big defenseman who detested all insects as much as most people hated venomous snakes.

I crawled into the whirlpool and closed my eyes, feeling better as I let the hot water bubble up all around me. Later, I went to take a shower.

"Hey, donkey-dick," Vlad said to Jonny Curtis, a prodigiously endowed player. "Your cock is so big, I bet when you get hard all the blood goes there and you pass out!"

"You'll never have that problem, Vlad." Curtis pointed at Vlad's micropenis.

"Is not what you have," Vlad said, red-faced with embarrassment, "is what you can do with it."

"That's not what your mum told me," I interjected as I left the showers and went to my locker.

Vlad shouted, "Fock you, Crossley! You asshole! Suck my balls, lick my ass!"

I got dressed, and as I started towards the locker room exit, Horton balled up his jersey and fired it at Pavel.

"Bastard! Don't you fuck with me!" Horton pointed an accusing finger at Pavel, who shrugged with a 'who, me?' expression. Then Horton gestured towards bits of cockroach on the floor. "Retarded fuckin' Russians." Horton shook his head and walked away.

By the time I left the building, the rain had completely let up. I joined half a dozen players who stood around someone's truck, drinking beer. We chattered with youthful exuberance and heehawed at each other's dirty jokes. Soon the refreshments ran out, and I stood there drinkless with Weston, Bourdin, Ignas and a couple of others. Most of us agreed to meet that evening at the Igloo.

"I won't be there," Barrie said, "because I have to speak to at some boys' club, but fill me in on whatever happens. I hate to miss a good party at the Igloo, and I bet you guys are going to have more fun tonight than I will."

I would go to the Igloo after stopping at Simon Kwan's house to replenish my supply of steroids and growth hormone pills. I also wanted to see Simon because Northup University had suspended him for participating in Occupy Bayporte. Simon, a scientist, environmentalist and broadcaster, had become admired in global entomological circles because of the papers he'd published about how to save bees. But his real success, according to him, had come as the host of *In Nature*, an internationally syndicated science-for-simpletons TV show.

The Canadian Civil Liberties Association had started pressuring

Northup to take him back, but Simon claimed that temporary unemployment suited him just fine, especially since the U. still sent him paychecks and he busied himself with interests he could pursue at home.

'I have something for you. Something that will help you," Simon had told me a year ago, when Jacques started ragging on me about my lack of strength and stamina. Simon's wise, kindly, open face and shock of white hair were so familiar to me and completely trustworthy. His eyes, the narrowest of dark slits, always seemed to see everything.

'I need your help,' I'd said.

'Then look here.' He'd shown me a bottle of liquid. He had other, similar bottles, plus vials of pills, arrayed on his bedroom dresser. I also saw boxes of syringes, needles and other injection paraphernalia. Winstrol, Deca, Equipoise. 'You know them as steroids,' he explained.

'Steroids,' I muttered, swallowing hard. "Bad stuff."

He smiled. 'Not so bad. You see these liquid bottles? They are for injection. The pills, of course, are to be swallowed, but the injections are far more beneficial. You train hard, eat sensibly and rest well then you take the steroids and growth hormone. You will be astounded at how much better your body responds to the exercise. Over time, you will become faster and stronger. You will have far more stamina. In the midseason or later, when everyone else is getting tired, you will still be vigorous and resilient. I can fix you up with the liquids, pills, syringes, needles—everything you need.'

'I'll have needle tracks all over my arms like a heroin addict,' I said.

He shook his head. 'Not in the arm. In the butt. It's difficult at first, but I'll show you how to do it. You may some help at first, because you have to do it right, but soon you'll be able to inject yourself and hardly feel any pain.'

'Why not just shoot it into my shoulder or leg?'

He shook his head. 'It would hurt, and it might interfere with your stick handling on the ice. The gluteus maximus is a very safe area for injecting steroids.' He began to prepare an injection. 'I will start you off with a little basic liquid testosterone combined with growth hormone. Drop your pants.'

I did as told, and felt the needle enter my right buttock. 'Ouch.'

'When you start injecting yourself,' he said as he angled the needle, 'you will learn to turn your leg to get a much better target, and you will become proficient at using each hand. You will need to learn to inject each buttock; one time the right side, the next time the left one.

'The liquids are best, and they come on two kinds: water-based and oil-based. The water-based steroids require a smaller-gauge needle. Each steroid has a different effect upon your body, and when you combine them with growth hormone...'

I smiled. A faster, stronger body through the use of these drugs! I had lifted weights harder than most of my teammates and yet placed last in strength. Other guys skated faster and stayed fresher, longer. Jacques, our head coach—that is, our boss—had said to me: I want to see some improvement if you want to keep playing for me. Simon finished the injection and assured me I could improve vastly as a hockey player. He went on about why they were invented, their chemical makeup, how to use them sensibly, which dosages to use, how to cycle on and off them, which ones did what for the body, which ones were good for strength or quick-muscle-twitch fiber or foot speed. I wanted only to get better and better at playing hockey. He said that steroids could help me become better than I ever thought I could be.

Once I got into steroids in a serious way, I would become a hockey machine. I could never slow down. Before me lay too much knowledge to absorb and retain, too many skills to master. I would have to concentrate hard on learning the technique of becoming a better skater. I would train the way no other hockey player ever had…and the world would be amazed.

So far, everything had worked out just fine.

Simon's spacious house, in a quaint, tree-lined part of town close to the campus, had become a hangout for the spoiled young malcontents of Bayporte. He shared his house for now with a couple of Northup students: an anthropology major from suburbia who had escaped from his overbearing parents; and a female theatre major who propositioned all visitors because she believed that having indiscriminate sex made her a better actress. I arrived near dinnertime and discovered the anthropology major sitting in the living room with his MacBook Pro on his stomach, typing complaints to his Internet friends about his parents' habit of ragging on him over his slovenly appearance and taste for dope. The theatre major, Anita, had moved to Bayporte from Calgary, where her father owned property, cattle and oil. She spent much of each day bitching that the Bayporte theatre community was "too uptight."

Simon sat in the living room, reading *Hustler* and listening to Joni Mitchell music. He had the TV turned on but the volume off.

"Hey, Simon," I said.

"Always nice to see you, Cross." He smiled as he got off the sofa and shook my hand. "I have what you need." He meant steroids and growth hormone pills. I still felt amazed that he could get us so much juice so often. He refused to tell me how he got it, though.

"You always come through for us," I said.

"My suppliers always come through for *me*."

"Mind if I make a cell call?"

"Step into the bedroom. More privacy."

I went into the bedroom, took out my iPhone and pressed a button. "Hi," I said.

"Hi yourself," Monique said. "Thanks for spending the night. I had fun."

"Me, too. Jacques hassled me this morning. What's going on with you?"

"My old man called to say he's still back east. He's flying back tonight. Want to come by for a quickie?"

"I'm at Simon's place now. I better not come over because Thornton might barge in on us. I'll check in with you tomorrow."

I ended the call and went back into the living room.

"Monique?" Simon asked. He knew about us and had offered us the use of his bedroom a few times.

"Yes." I felt glad to be here at Simon's, getting our crucial and illicit business out of the way. "So, how goes your struggle against oppression?"

He shrugged. "We're slowly making progress. I'm expecting some kids to come by and share their latest ideas on how to save the world from hypocrisy. They all want to become lobbyists with big paychecks and two-hour lunches."

"No hypocrisy there," I said as we wandered into the kitchen.

Simon had become a leader of the school's libertarian movement, even though libertarianism by definition rejected the concept of leadership. He'd probably become a political iconoclast just to piss off his bosses at huge, old, staid Northup. Once called "the Harvard of Canada" by the college guidebooks, Northup had looted its arts and humanities departments in order to improve its research and faculty in science, engineering and agriculture.

"The main thing I've learned about these young people," Simon once said, speaking of the Bayporte wanderers, outcasts and latent terrorists he met every week, "is how similar they are to their parents. They like their goodies as much as their mums and dads do. Frank Zappa once said, 'If your kids knew how lame you really were, they would kill you in your sleep.' I would say, 'Kids, if you knew just how much like your lame parents *you* were, you would kill yourselves right now.'"

Simon's favorite things were marijuana, music, college women and whatever else made him feel good for a while. He saw much value in the rhetoric of the antiwar 1960s—that everybody should be free to go his own way and do his own thing. But he also knew that those who had the gold made the rules.

"Hungry?" he asked now as he stood at the stove, stirring a big pot of something brown and smelly.

"What is it?" I asked.

"I'm not sure." Simon cooked and ate some very peculiar foods.

Anita came into the room. In her early twenties, she had long, dirty blonde hair, a doper's paunch and bubble butt. Her small breasts swung freely inside her old T-shirt. Her clear skin and big, friendly smile made me feel sad that a potentially pretty girl like her made such an effort to look homely.

"Hey, Cross," she said, distracted.

"Hello, Anita," She'd tried to get into my pants a few times, but I said no, because I suspected her to be a very repressed little girl pretending to be liberated. When she first met Barrie, she said, "Hi! Let's fuck!" He said OK, and they went upstairs. Later, he said, 'She disappointed me. No fellatio or cunnilingus. Frigid little bitch, too. Afterwards, she called me a selfish prick. When I went to leave, she body-blocked me at the door. She's stronger than she looks. However, because of the steroids, I wrestled her out of my way. I hope Simon never turns *her* on to juice.'

"Simon," she said now, "You know I have some friends coming in from out of town and I don't think they have taxi fare from the bus station. I want to pick them up." She sounded like a little kid trying to wheedle movie money out of her daddy. "I need to use your car."

"Are you asking me or telling me?"

She paused. "I'm asking."

"Then *ask*."

Anita sighed and nodded. "Simon, may I borrow your car?"

Simon smiled. "That wasn't so hard, was it? Yes, you may." He tossed her the keys; she flashed him a thanks-a-million smile and fled out the door.

"Simon," I said, "you know what your problem is? You're just too nice a guy."

"I know. I need to toughen up and start saying no to these young people who adore me so much." He stirred the dinner some more. "I'm always hungry, too. This'll be ready in a few minutes."

"I'm going to watch some TV," I said. In the living room, I plopped down onto the sofa and stared at the cartoons, trying to read the characters' lips. I dozed off and felt myself being shaken awake.

"Anita has returned," Simon announced, standing over me. "You should come into the kitchen and meet her friends."

"Eh?"

"Anita and her friends. Her friends are from out of town. They're in the kitchen. Come say hi."

"Oh. Yeah. Gotta say hi."

"They're into raging against the machine and establishing a new world order," he told me.

"Nice for them."

"They think men are scum."

"So do I." Laughing, we went into the kitchen.

Four young females sat at the big, sticky kitchen table.

"This is Christopher," Simon told them.

Anita smiled again. The female next to her, whose Army surplus jacket bore the stenciled name Grant, glanced a bit in our direction. The others paid us no notice at all.

Grant began rolling a joint. "So, what's your thing?" she asked me.

"Excuse me?" I replied.

"What's your thing, man?" Grant repeated, annoyed. "What's your gig? Like, do you have a job?"

"I'm an entertainer," I said.

"Do you act? Sing? Dance?" Grant asked.

"No. I'm in sports. Pro sports."

"Which sport?"

"I play hockey."

"What's your team?"

"The Bayporte Bullies."

Grant made a face. "Yuck."

One of the other girls guffawed. "Yeah, right! I get it! You're an entertainer! Hockey is entertainment for people without meaning or purpose in life!"

My iPhone rang in my pocket. I took it out and said hello.

"Cross, this is Barrie. You remember that speaking thing I had today at the boys' club? I was hoping to wrap it up early and meet up with you at the Igloo, but no can do. We'll talk tomorrow. Maybe I'll have some adventures to tell you about." Click.

"So," Grant was saying, "I told the pig, 'Your badge and gun don't scare me.' You have to stand up to them or they'll Taser your ass."

"Ooh! That would be awful," Anita said.

"Come with me." Simon walked me down the hallway into his bedroom. In his dresser were small bottles of liquid. He took one out. "What's your current regimen?"

"One injectable and one oral."

"Oil-based injectable?" he asked. "Twice weekly?"

"Affirmative."

Simon nodded. His shock of white hair and matching goatee looked like cotton candy. "You've made significant progress in the time you've been using these products, and you can improve even more."

"Good to know," I said.

"I want you to start frontloading and kickstarting."

"Sounds like fun. Tell more more."

"A frontload means taking twice as much as usual so that your blood concentration levels will be much higher much faster. An oral kickstart means taking a fast-acting pill until your injections reach their peak. I'll give you some anti-estrogens so you won't have any humiliating side effects."

"Bitch tits?"

He smiled. "Exactly. How are Barrie, Ignas, Bourdin and those guys doing?"

"Oh, they love their meds, just like me."

Simon kept meticulous records about us and our juice but refused to sell them to anyone but me, so I acted as the middleman between Simon and my teammates. "My supplier, Simon Kwan, is one of the most famous and respected men in Canada."

Simon laughed. "Where would the Bullies be without me?"

"Nowhere, on our way to no place."

I could hear the Grateful Dead playing something groovy and bluesy on the stereo. "Take it easy on the pills and tablets, because they can destroy your liver," Simon reminded me. "Nobody's tipped you off to an upcoming 'no notice' urine test?"

I shook my head. "No, but Jacques called me in and we had a little chat about this very subject. He asked me to keep my eyes and ears open for Bullies on juice and report to him if I see or hear anything he should know about."

"Good luck with that, Jacques," Simon muttered. "I heard some retired NHL player on TV the other day say something to the effect of, 'There are no steroids in the NHL, period. There may have been some of that stuff happening in the 'Eighties and 'Nineties, but not now.' If they really clamped down and tested everyone and they used very sensitive, reliable methods, I wonder how many quality players they would have left."

We finished up our business, I thanked Simon and headed out the door. In my car, I noticed right away that someone had tampered with my glove compartment but taken nothing. I stored my cannabis and juice in the trunk, revved up my BMW and drove in the direction of the Igloo. I made a left at Yukon Road, turned onto Campus Boulevard and, minutes later, arrived at Northup University. I admired the pretty young women in their sweatshirts, skintight Levi's and Nikes, knapsacks slung over their shoulders. Youthful and exuberant, all smiles, they looked to me as magnificent as dewy animals striding along the countryside. I had a hard time believing that, not so long ago, I had been a student here; yet my memories of this place and its people seemed like sepia-tinted images floating about in my mind's eye.

But I remembered her with ease. I fell for her braided hair, suburban clothes and teen-queen beauty. Inspired by her efforts at looking fashionable, I started wearing blazers, pleated slacks and high-top runners. I had no fraternity patch or other decoration designating me as someone special; my Grizzlies warmup jacket, worn only by players, meant nothing to her.

She wanted me to go Greek. I nearly did. I pledged to Omega Delta Chi, but common sense prevented me from subjecting myself to the insanity of Hell Week. I didn't want arts majors from Winnipeg or coaches-in-training from Newfoundland torturing me just so that they would deem me acceptable to move into their overpopulated, stinky house. They had even assigned me a Big Brother, my fraternity mentor—his name was Eddie—who phoned me each night with passionate pleas to come over and party with the boys. I demurred, more out of indolence than anything else. Eddie's offer of lifelong friendship moved me, though, especially his profound regret over my passing up an opportunity to become roommates with "tomorrow's leaders."

Soon after rejecting Omega Delta Chi, I sat in Northup's huge campus pub, comfortable in the section informally reserved for jocks, when Eddie and some of the other Greeks cruised in with their women and settled into the corner unofficially theirs. Thrilled to see Eddie again, I got up and ambled over to say hello.

Eddie and his companions saw me coming, and none of them smiled as I made my approach. I went up to him and offered him my most jovial of handshakes. He got up and, before either of us had spoken, threw a feeble right cross that I easily slapped away. But he kept at me, vicious and relentless, like an underdog boxer punching it out for a million-dollar purse.

Eddie couldn't take me, of course, since I had six inches and forty pounds on him, but his wimpy little attack confused and humiliated more than angered me. I could practically hear the lactic acid seeping into his arms, paralyzing him. Exhausted, he slumped back onto his seat and cried, "You asshole! You made me look like a fool when you wouldn't join up!"

I told him that Greek life and I were incompatible, and that my rejection of the fraternity had been my loss, not his. I also wanted to tell him to grow up and stop picking fights with guys who could break him in half.

Now, driving through Northup, I started to see things a bit more clearly. If someone gets desperate enough for the approval of others, he will drink beer until he vomits, or he will allow gay music majors from Regina spank his ass with a ping pong paddle. He will even walk around on campus dressed only in a brassiere and panties as January snowflakes freeze his shoulders. He does these things for the opportunity of being lifelong friends with a group of guys who will forget about him after graduation.

Really, how can he respect himself after being degraded by people claiming to be his friends, especially when he recognizes that his fraternity days have become a mere memory and source of colorful stories? Now he is an adult, in middle age, alone and lonely. What is he to make of it all?

I stopped to allow a few girls to cross the street so they could get to the student union building. They were dressed in Northup chic: sweatshirts, jeans, boots. One of them, much prettier than the others, wore a baseball cap and had long, flowing blonde hair.

I gazed at them as they walked by me. The blonde girl looked straight at me, and I looked back at her. I smiled; she looked away, perhaps affronted that I would try to engage her in a moment's intimacy. If I had been her age, and driving a secondhand subcompact, would she have smiled? I hated to admit that college girls didn't smile at me anymore unless they recognized me, and when they did speak to me, they called me sir.

I didn't belong to her world, but so what? I had never been a joiner, anyway.

I turned onto Beach Road and drove by the house I had shared with my wife during our brief, disastrous marriage. My own complacency had spared me from the horrors of Greek life, but simple lust had been responsible for my many hours with her in that creaking, aging Volvo of hers, making it rock back and forth in the sorority parking lot. Soon after moving into our new house, I arrived home and discovered her naked on the sofa with Pavel. The only good thing I could say about that guy was that he got me out of my miserable marriage.

Our divorce, quick but nasty, resulted in her keeping everything she had and getting most of my assets. It turned out that half the Bullies had screwed my wife, and Warren Gotch wanted to trade me to Anaheim because of the attention the media gave to my private life. I wondered if Barrie Weston had *shtupped* my missus; he said no. My wife claimed that I loved Barrie more than I did her; maybe she knew me better than I did.

I made it downtown without remembering how I'd gotten there, and spotted the Igloo's big penguin sign. A big white dome of a building, the Igloo had been the place where my grandparents went ice skating after World War Two. Its owners converted it into a highly popular nightclub in the 1980s. Soon, they would probably sell it to real estate developers who wanted to knock it down and replace it with a condominium.

Its marquee said, "A Tribute to Michael Jackson."

"Mr. Cross?" asked the doorman. "They're expecting you inside."

Inside, the manager, a big man in a loud, dark suit regarded me with the look of a long-lost love. I feared he would hug and kiss me.

"Your party's inside," he said. "You guys going to win it all this year? Hey?"

"Yeah, all the way!" I nodded with a little fist pump, then hurried into the darkened showroom. The sound of laughter drew me towards Donny Bourdin and his crowd. Soon I found Donny, sitting with several others. The server took our orders. I asked for a Sprite.

"What? Sprite?" Donny nearly screamed. "I thought you'd want some *juice!* Get it?"

Denis Pilon slid under the table. "Watch out! Crossley has a gun! He'll kill us all!" His childish antics made me giggle, but no one else showed any amusement. Then the stage lights brightened and an unseen emcee announced, "Get ready for our tribute to the late, great Michael Jackson!" The opening notes of *Billie Jean* thumped through the room and the curtains parted. A skinny dark man stood before us in a sequined black jacket and black slacks. He wore Day-Glo white socks, patent-leather black shoes and a white glove. He grabbed his balls and pumped his ass. He didn't really look like Michael Jackson. I thought he looked more like Prince, or maybe Liza Minnelli.

Denis Pilon, still mostly under the table, peered around at us, then hopped onto his seat, stood up and belted out a rock-star scream: *"Yeeaaahhh!"*

Michael Jackson, like the rest of us, at first felt startled by the scream, then pointed and smiled at the hockey player. Pilon screamed again, and everyone laughed except his date. She grabbed at his ankle and motioned for him to sit.

Michael Jackson's next song, also from *Thriller*, started up. I looked at the rear of the Igloo and saw Pat Paterson enter with Laurel English. They took a table at the other side of the room, and I could have sworn that she smiled at me.

Michael Jackson finished his song to wild applause. Our group cheered for him and Pilon screamed some more. Then Sean Marcelin left his two dates, sidled up next to Donny and started whispering to him. Donny ordered more drinks, reached into his pocket and withdrew a cigarette lighter. He held its flame under Marcelin's chin for a moment.

"Hothead!" Donny screamed. He and Denis Pilon both burst out laughing. The women all shuddered as Marcelin rubbed at his reddened chin.

"Fuck you, Donny!" Marcelin shouted. He dunked a napkin into one of the cocktail glasses and dabbed it at where he'd been burned. "You're so mean."

Ignas, his date and Jonny Curtis got up and said they were expected at another nightclub that evening. They said goodnight and disappeared.

"Hothead!" Bourdin yelled again as he stuck his lighter under Pilon's chin. Pilon pushed his hand away, and Bourdin knocked a drink into the lap of Barbara Charlton, the woman he loved.

"Yuck!" Barbara said, reaching for a napkin to dry herself off. "Donny! You're such an…I don't know what!"

"Get off the rag," Bourdin said.

"What did you say?" Barbara asked, glowering.

"Get off the rag." He leaned over and stared into her eyes. "Get off the rag."

She swallowed hard and looked around. She tried to rise and run, but Donny grabbed a handful of her hair and kept her still. Barbara sat, looking down, her face morose. Bourdin kept holding onto her hair and seemed to be pulling it, but she said nothing. Presently he let go and she burst into tears.

I thought, Barbara, you poor thing. You've finally gotten to see your man act like a pig.

Bourdin raised his glass in a toasting gesture and screamed. Pilon did likewise.

"Get off the rag, bitches!" the two grown men cried out in unison. Both roared with laughter.

More cocktails arrived, Bourdin put away his lighter, and we did our best to pretend that no chins had been burned, drinks spilled or feelings bruised. As I got up to leave the table, I observed Bourdin reaching for his cigarette lighter and eyeing Pilon. I hustled off.

Laurel and Paterson had a table at the back. They had an extra chair, so I occupied it without being invited to do so. Paterson beamed at me. "Cross! Great to see you! How's it goin'?"

"Doing fine," I said, wishing he would be a true gentleman and get lost so I could hit on his date.

"Laurel," he said to Laurel, "this is Chris Crossman."

"Crossley." I offered Laurel a brief wave. "Call me Cross."

"Hey?" Paterson looked confused. "Yes, now I remember. Chris Cross. He plays hockey for our team."

"I believe we've met once or twice," she said.

"The reason I came over," I lied to Paterson, "is to invite you to our table over by the stage."

"Terrific!" Paterson grabbed his drink and stood up. "I've been wanting to talk to Donny and Denis about some business." He looked at Laurel. "Well...?"

"You go ahead. I'll join you a bit later."

"We'll both join you," I said.

"Sounds good." Paterson hurried off towards the noisy table. As he passed by, I saw the glint of a holstered handgun inside of his suit coat.

"Why," I asked Laurel, "do you date him?"

"Why do *you* spend so much time with those Neanderthals?"

"Because I have to."

Paterson sat with those Neanderthals now, grinning and shaking hands.

"Why does an entrepreneur, or whatever he calls himself, need to carry a piece?" I asked.

"I guess he thinks it for self-defense."

Soon we heard wild laughter plus the clinking and shattering of cocktail glasses.

"What are they doing?" Laurel asked.

"Hothead," I said.

"What's a 'hothead'?"

"They hold a flame under each other's chin. The guy who gets the worst third-degree burns wins."

Laurel cringed. "That's horrible."

"I agree. Fortunately, I'm too far away to get a hothead." Then, "I'm just wondering about something: Do I make you uncomfortable?"

"No," she said, too fast. After a long pause, she added, "You seem a bit creepy sometimes. I remember you from another get-together."

"We met at Donny's party."

She shook her head. "No, it was here at the Igloo. You were here with Darcie Chapman. You were checking out the other women. A lot."

"Do you want to know why?"

"Not particularly," Laurel said.

"I'll tell you anyway. I wasn't her type. She liked other women."

"Too bad for her."

"No, too bad for *me*."

We heard a commotion and looked around. Denis Pilon, on stage, had just started doing a drunken striptease. His date and some of the servers seemed disturbed by the spectacle, but everyone else just sat, waiting to see what the big, handsome wild man would do next. A couple of bouncers hurried over to the stage, but Donny Bourdin, standing guard there, pushed them backwards. The bouncers went sprawling and hit some servers, and they all lay scattered about like toppled bowling pins.

Pilon had taken off most of his clothes, balled up each item and fired it at his date, who sat still as the garments struck her. Naked, he began pulling on his penis, then pointing it at different customers, who ducked to avoid being sprayed. Then he started pointing his dick at his date, who sat with her head down and eyes closed.

"Get off the rag, bitch!" he screamed like a banshee. "Be a goddamn woman and get off the rag!"

He bounded off the stage, headed straight for her and began slapping her. People ran to her aid but Bourdin shoved them away.

"I've had enough," Laurel said, getting up.

"Come with me," I said, grabbing her hand as I sprinted for the door. Minutes later, we were in my car, eastbound on Central Avenue, both of us staying silent for some time.

"Turn back," Laurel finally said. "Pat is still there. He'll be worrying about me."

"No, he won't. He'll be worrying about what the cops will do if they see his gun."

"The cops? Really?"

"With that scene? Yeah, the manager would have called in the boys in blue the moment Bourdin started beating up on the bouncers."

"Well, then, you better drive me home," she said.

"Where do you live?"

"In Whitley."

I frowned. "That's way the hell out there in the Valley."

"If Whitley's too much trouble, you can just drive me back to the Igloo."

"Whitley it is." Soon we were on the freeway, heading for the distant town that had gone from being a Canadian military base to a bedroom community.

"Were you born and raised in Whitley?" I asked, checking my rearview mirror to make sure the cops weren't behind me.

"No. I moved there because of my husband," she said.

My heart sank. Husband? Shit.

"He was killed near Kabul a few years ago," she continued. "In case you were wondering."

"I'm sorry to hear that."

"I doubt it. But it's nice of you to say so. He hated the war as much as everybody else did, but he felt he owed it to Canada to be there and make himself useful."

"I would never join the military," I told her. "If I had been an American during the Vietnam years, I would've run off to Canada. Let the FBI come up here and try to drag me back to the States."

"He was in Kabul," she went on, "when he decided he'd finally had enough. He had been a career officer, and for the first time wondered if he was on the right side of a conflict. He couldn't make sense of why we were in Afghanistan, so he decided to retire and come home.

While they were processing his file, he was killed."

"War!" I sang out, pounding on the steering wheel. "What can it be good for? Absolutely nothing!" I wanted to put on the satellite radio and zone out on some music but Laurel might have considered me rude.

"Don't feel too badly about my widowhood," she said. "I've mostly gotten over it. I'm not wearing black all the time and wishing I would die and join him in the hereafter. He was a good guy. Maybe we would have had a long and happy life together. Or maybe not. Anyway, he was in uniform the first time we met, and there was all this awful stuff going on in Iraq and Afghanistan. So he knew his deployment over there was inevitable, and we talked all the time about when his overseas work was done and he came home, what kind of life we wanted to have then. But then he went over and the experience really traumatized him. It traumatized me, too. I cried all the time because he would either get killed over there or maybe get so shell-shocked that he wouldn't be the same man I'd married. So, when I learned that he had been killed, I told myself that I had a choice: I could mourn him for the rest of my life or try to be happy and enjoy myself."

I smiled. "You made the right choice." I looked straight ahead. We had left Bayporte and were entering the Valley, an endless place of hills, mountains and farmland.

"Please drive carefully out here," she said.

"I hear ya." I kept both hands on the steering wheel and slowed down a bit. "I remember when I came of age and started going to Northup. I had to ask myself if I wanted to put all my energy into hockey or get a more conventional education." I kept looking over at her and swerving a bit.

"Please drive carefully," she repeated.

"Yeah, sure. Anyway, I learned the value of setting realistic goals and always attaining those goals."

"My goal is to get home safely," she said, her voice anxious. "I'm not sure how realistic that is, either, with the way you're driving."

"My apologies. Anyway, it may sound stupid to say that a teenager would have this 'I will not fail' attitude, but when you're a teenage boy, you can be really cocky. I got my braces off and my skin cleared up. I got laid a few times and Northup came through with a full hockey scholarship. I was young and all things seemed possible. What did you do during *your* misspent youth?"

"I wore my hair down to my butt and made friends with all the people my parents warned me about."

"And how did *that* turn out?"

"I got knocked up," she said. "I was fifteen."

"Wow," I said. "Tell me more."

"You would have liked me then. I was an easy lay. Then the doc told me I was 'expecting,' and that made me grow up just a little bit. I had to do some soul searching.

"My parents and I fought like hell about this. The father of my unborn child didn't know I was pregnant. My parents always insisted on making my decisions for me, and I mean *all* my decisions, even the small ones. I guess all parents are on a power trip about running their kids' lives. They wanted me to get an abortion. I didn't want to have a kid, but I damn sure didn't want Mummy and Daddy telling me what to do about this. I told I was going to keep my baby, and if they didn't like it, too bad.

"The baby was stillborn. The doc told me so and I just said, 'Really? My baby's toast, eh? Can I go home now?'"

"You took it very well," I told her.

"I've always coped well with adversity," she said.

"Maybe your higher power meant for you to be driving with a handsome man through the Canadian wilderness on this night."

"Turn right here."

I got off the freeway and soon we arrived at her driveway. I saw a young Indian or Pakistani man in work clothes.

"Laurel?" he called out.

"Hi, Jaspal. A friend drove me home. Want to come inside with us?"

"OK." He opened the gate and got into the back seat of my car. "Jaspal Singh," he said, reaching past Laurel to shake my hand.

"Chris Crossley," I said, shaking his hand. He had a firm grip and an open, friendly smile.

"The Bully?" he asked.

"I'm also a liar, a thief and a womanizer."

He laughed. "Well, I like seeing you score those goals."

"Me too. It beats the hell out of sitting on the bench."

The car's lights were still on and I looked around. From what I could see, Laurel had quite a spread. Two big black Labrador retrievers emerged, wagging their tails.

I killed the engine and got out of the car. The three of us went to the back of the house and into the kitchen.

"Jaspal," Laurel said, "take Cross into the living room. I'll put tea on."

Her immense living room had walls of stone and a floor of gleaming hardwood. Her sofas were huge and so were her wrought-iron coffee tables. Jaspal began loading fat logs into the fireplace. Then he lit them up and they crackled to life. The heat felt wonderful.

"In case you were wondering," he said, "I'm not Laurel's lover. She and I were school friends. When her husband went to Afghanistan, I moved in at her request. She didn't want to be here by herself and her husband's people were assholes. They came by for a visit, but when they saw me and realized I was living here with her, they left very quickly and didn't come back. They didn't bother to attend his memorial service." Jaspal spoke perfect, unaccented English.

"To hell with them," I said, feeling the heat of the fire wash all over me. The flames danced. I wanted to get up and dance with them.

"Cross, I envy you because you have a great sports career. Is it fun for you?"

"It has its moments. I've gotten some shit from the sports media, but it's better than selling real estate, which is what many washed-up hockey players do."

"I wanted to play hockey. I did it when I was a teenager, but I just didn't have the size, strength or killer instinct for the NHL." Jaspal, tall and muscular, probably had a point about lacking the killer instinct. Much too nice a guy.

"Killer instinct," I murmured as I sat staring at the fire.

"I didn't want to give or get a concussion," he said.

"Me neither."

Jaspal smirked. "But it happens."

I nodded. "Far too often."

He looked at my arms as we sat in the darkness while the fire crackled. "You have a big set of guns."

"We all do, on our team. We lift weights like maniacs. We have specially designed exercises to promote muscle development."

He grinned. "And big, nutritious meals."

"There's that, too."

His eyes narrowed a bit. "Is that all? Aren't there other things?"

"Like what?"

His grin disappeared. "Oh, I think you know. Whenever the subject comes up about steroids and human growth hormones and the rest of it, the Bullies are the first team mentioned."

I raised my chin a bit. "We do our best to maintain our integrity." For a moment I wished I could be a mere ranch hand like Jaspal. Let him shoot the juice and score the goals.

Integrity. Tom Brennan had used that word at the players' meeting earlier that year. Each team's captain and alternate had traveled to Philadelphia for a discussion of performance-enhancing drugs in professional sports. The NHL, always claiming to be a drug-free zone, nevertheless wished to educate it players on what this highly controversial subject.

"Integrity. That is what this meeting is all about," Brennan had told us. "The integrity of the NHL is far more important than the statistics of any individual player. That's why I am so proud to stand before all of you as the president of the players' association."

Tom Brennan had played for San Jose for ten seasons. He had served as our association's president for three or four years. "I am pleased to see so many players here, especially the captains and alternates from the postseason teams. I think it's crucial to show that all teams are taking this matter seriously. I see the Bullies' Barrie Weston here. Barrie, would you mind saying a few words to us now about how the Bayporte guys feel?"

Brennan pointed to the back of the room, where Barrie and I stood, jetlagged and cranky. We had arrived in Philly and gone out with a magazine reporter doing a story on Barrie. After getting a few hours' sleep, we stumbled into the meeting, and now Barrie cleared his throat to tell all the guys how the Bayporte juicers felt about steroids in the NHL.

"Well, first, let me say that standing next to me is Chris Cross"—I offered everyone a wave and smile—"and I want to assure everyone here that the Bullies are taking this drug issue very seriously and we're prepared to maintain our integrity." He nodded and everyone applauded.

"Thank you, Barrie." Tom Brennan wore a dark suit and sober tie that made him look more like a lawyer than a hockey players' representative. "Now, before we continue, I want to talk about a bastard who's been trying to make some trouble for us. I won't dignify him by saying his name, but I'm sure everyone here knows who I'm talking about. That little fucker has been going on Twitter and Facebook and indicating that he used performance-enhancing drugs while playing and is going to write a tell-all book about steroids in the NHL." Brennan shook his head, clenching his fists. "Well, that asshole has been saying these things and I'm not going to forget or forgive. If I run into him, I'll pound him, I swear to God. I'll teach him not to treat us like that." He looked for a moment as if he would slam his fist into something or someone, then he settled down a bit. "All right, I have a PowerPoint presentation ready. Let's take a close look at steroids and growth hormones so we can get a clear picture of our enemies…"

The rest of the meeting was a boring series of slides: syringes and needles, pill bottles, bitch tits and zits. I felt like a high school kid in guidance class enduring a "just say no" presentation.

That evening, Weston, Brennan and some others went out to dinner. I sat alone in a bar when my iPhone rang.

"Cross, this is Phil Brady. Is Barrie there? I need to speak to him." Phil Brady, our former second-string goalie, worked as Roderick Rainey's promotions manager.

"Barrie is not here," I said.

"Roderick is totally pissed off. He knows about that meeting you're at, and the sports media here are reporting that you guys are in Philly trying to find ways of circumventing the drug tests."

I chortled. "We had a meeting, but it wasn't about dodging the piss tests."

"Well, whatever happened at that meeting, Roderick's all worked up about it. He fired me this afternoon! Shit! What will I do now?"

"I'm sorry to hear that, Phil. But I've already assured Roderick we're not juicing, and if you'll give him a chance to cool off, I'm sure he'll rehire you. If he doesn't, well, maybe you're better off without that job."

"That's the dumbest thing I've ever heard, you dipshit. You're to blame for my termination. You had no business sneaking off to Philadelphia like that."

"Brady, I don't have to listen to this crap." I hung up the phone.

Moments later, my phone rang again. "Crossley, if you hang up on me again—"

Click.

It rang once more, and against my better judgment, I answered it.

"Now, Cross, this is getting expensive, so please just hear me out. You need to call Roderick and tell him that I'm a good guy. I need to get my job back. I've never been so underworked and overpaid in my life." He choked back a sob.

"Shit, Phil." I looked around the dark, cozy bar and hoped nobody could overhear my conversation. "I'm not sure what I could tell Roderick that would do you any good. He thinks I'm a born fucking liar, which I probably am."

"Just tell him that you guys aren't using steroids and that if I discovered you using them, I would be the first person to tell him." I could hear him snuffling over the phone.

"All right, Phil, I'll do that. Just stop blubbering, will you?"

Brady gave me Roderick's home number, which I already had; after all, Roderick wanted to adopt me. I tried to call him but got no answer. When I saw Barrie again in our hotel room, I told him about Phil's phone calls but he said he didn't care about Phil's predicament. After a long, refreshing night's sleep, I mostly forgot about it, too.

They canceled the following day's meeting because someone had made off with some of the association's computer disks. Brennan learned that Warren Gotch had flown in to spy on the meetings; bursting into Gotcha's hotel room, Brennan discovered the Bullies' general manager copying the disks and emailing them to Roderick. Gotcha's two assistants had to restrain Brennan, who threatened to rip out Gotcha's jugular if the two men ever ended up in the same room or dark alley alone. Warren issued a statement that someone had found the disks, presented them to him, and he merely wanted to locate their rightful owner.

Nothing really came of those meetings, although Phil Brady got his job back, and some months later an investigation revealed that Tom Brennan had used players' association funds for gambling and prostitutes.

"Integrity," I muttered, sitting on Laurel's floor.

"Did you say something?" Jaspal asked.

"Just talking to myself. Thinking about integrity."

"Well," he said, "if you don't have integrity, you don't have anything at all."

I shrugged and thought again about that meeting in Philadelphia. I had a nice time and ate some good cheesesteaks, and we all agreed: people shouldn't stick needles in their asses and flood their bodies with synthetic testosterone.

"Do you like the ranch?" Jaspal asked. "It *is* a ranch, you know. Laurel's husband left her well off, so she doesn't really need to work or do much of anything else. But she likes to do things and stay busy. We raise and sell cows on a small scale."

"Who's your resident photographer?" I asked.

"Photographer?" Laurel asked, entering the room with a tray for tea.

"Yeah, photographer. Might be nice to take pictures of the cows before you sell them. No two cows look exactly alike." I grinned.

"Every farm should have a portrait photographer. I'd like to have a job like that after I retire from hockey."

"Taking pictures of cows?" Laurel asked, incredulous. "How about some tea? It'll give you something to do think about aside from hockey, Igloo fights and photographing livestock."

Dogs started barking. Jaspal said, "I should lock up for the night."

He left, and Laurel said, "Jaspal is a poet, you know. One of the best I've ever read."

"Nice guy," I said. For several moments, we stared at each other. She looked ethereal, beautiful. She also seemed tragic, lonely. I got up and walked around for a minute, then sat back down. I heard the door close, looked up and felt glad to see Jaspal standing there.

"All's clear," he said. "I'm off to bed."

"Good night, Jaspal," Laurel said. "And thank you."

"Does he live in the guest house?" I asked.

"Yes," she answered. "He writes his poetry there."

"Sounds like a good arrangement," I said.

"It's a great arrangement."

"And Pat Paterson. What about him? Is *he* part of your arrangement, too?"

Her eyes narrowed. "Not that kind of relationship. Frankly, I think he wants to do business with me. Everyone can see that I'm not exactly poor, and he wants to surround himself with affluent people who will invest their money with him." She paused. "I don't want to see him again. He said some insensitive things about Jaspal tonight while we were heading for the Igloo."

"Pat is a goof."

"He thinks you're OK," she said.

"Does he? He's always saying, 'Call me. We'll do some deals.' You're better off without him."

"How come *you're* not married?" she asked. "Got a girl?"

"I'm divorced. It's an old story: poor boy from wrong side of Bayporte gets hockey scholarship, marries rich sorority girl who gets bored with him and starts cheating on him. Then *he* gets shaken down in divorce court."

We stayed quiet for a few minutes. Then she asked, "Want to get high?"

"Always," I answered.

Nodding, Laurel got up and walked away. She returned with a tin can. She had also changed into jeans and a T-shirt. We settled on the floor together and she rolled a joint. After taking a big hit, she handed it to me. Soon I started to feel the relaxing warmth of cannabis.

"Mmmm," I said. "So good..."

"My husband sent me a whole shipment," she said, "in an empty coffin from Afghanistan. Isn't that awful?" She wrinkled up her nose and let out a giggly little doper's laugh.

"A coffin," I murmured. "Afghan dope. Too weird." I got to my feet and walked to the window. Six, or sixty, Taliban snipers covered the house in standard two-by-two cover formation.

"What do you do?" I asked, not looking at her and not bothering to add anything to my question. The Taliban, or whoever they were, looked like a bunch of little Osama bin Ladens in caps and flowing gowns. Kill the Taliban, I thought. Kill them dead.

"What do I do?" She considered my question. "Jim Morrison once said, 'I just want to get fat, do nothing and go nowhere. Just be.' I like that answer."

"Mostly you just do your own thing," I said.

She smiled. "I like it that way. I'm happier than most people I know."

I moved over and sat down right next to her. I took a huge hit of the joint and pressed my mouth to hers, blowing smoke into her lungs. I pulled at her T-shirt. She flinched, then sat back and let me pull off her clothes. I kissed her and she kissed back. She got up, naked, and went away. She came back with what looked like a big sleeping bag and lay it close to the fire. I crawled on top of her.

We made love to each other for eons. The dope made it a transcendental experience. When the fire died, I threw in more logs and made it come alive again. I felt alive again, too. I looked into the fire, seeing nothing and everything. I crawled back to Laurel and we lay together. I dreamed of good things, then bad things. When the bad things got worse, I woke up, unsure of my surroundings.

My head ached a little bit. The clock said four-thirty in the morning. I felt muzzy; next to me, Laurel slept, serene and beautiful. I gazed at her and wanted to go back to sleep, to cuddle her forever in this big, fine old room. I wondered what we expected from each other now. The fire had died again and the room felt chilly. What happened to the life and fire that had consumed our senses just a few hours earlier? Could we get it back, or had it just faded away, like everything else?

I believed in the falseness of everything and the truth of nothing. Only occasionally can we get past the falseness and see the truth. The periods when we *are* real and true are brief because they have to be. My time for being real with Laurel had ended, so I got dressed and returned to the illusion of being Chris Cross.

Outside, the sky remained dark and even the birds were still asleep. I got into my car and stared out the windshield, looking at Laurel's beautiful, fake house.

The day struggled to break on through.

Well, I thought, bring it on, motherfucker.

4

The darkness had only barely lifted when I pulled into a roadside restaurant. I placed my order, turned on my iPad and chugged down some coffee. In the headlines, our premier said she wanted to find ways to aid the city's homeless while some real estate developers tried to buy the blocks of skid row hotels, convert them into condominiums and sell them to well-paid city dwellers. I didn't care about the sports reports unless they mentioned me, and even then I cared very little.

I devoured my All-Canadian Breakfast Special: two scrambled eggs, hash browns, bacon and toast. I drank some more coffee and paid the check, then went back to my car. The sky had lightened up and the dawn air smelled of gasoline. I got in and drove, paying no attention to my speed. So I nearly had a heart attack when I noticed the flashing lights directly behind me. I put on my turn signal, pulled over to the side of the road and started digging for my driver's license. By the time the Royal Canadian Mounted Police officer reached me, I had my hand out, sticking my license at him.

"Please step out of your vehicle, sir," he said.

Oh, no, I thought. Please don't search my car. We both walked with care as cars and trucks zoomed past us. The Mountie and I stood by his car as he studied my license.

"Where were you born?" he asked.

"I don't remember. I was very young at the time."

He frowned. "Getting smart with me, eh?"

"I was born in Bayporte," I said.

"I clocked you at one hundred ten, Wallace."

I was born Wallace Christopher Crossley, but I try not to think about that very often.

"I apologize for that, Constable. It won't happen again," I said.

The cop looked at me for the longest time. I ran a hand through my messy hair. I really hoped he wouldn't search my car.

"Have you had anything to drink in the past few hours?" he asked.

"No, sir. I've been driving all night. I'm just on my way home to get some sleep."

The cop frowned again and nodded, as if I had just given him a complicated legal answer and he needed a few minutes to sort it all out. He gave me back my license and smiled.

"OK, Cross, get some sleep. We need you to be well rested when the postseason starts."

"Yes, Constable, I'll do my best."

"Are you guys all ready to go back east and take on the Rangers?"

I nodded and smiled.

"Get us a Stanley Cup, hey? Do you think you could get tickets for me and my girlfriend?"

"Yeah. Just call me a few or so beforehand and I'll fix you up." I shook his hand. "Nice to meet you."

"Do me a favor. Be careful out there. We've been getting bad press lately, and it would be too bad if Chris Cross got squashed all over the road on my watch."

I got back into my car and resumed my journey. Sunrise began as I pulled into the parking lot of our practice facility. Barrie had gotten in even though they had locked the place and he had no key. I knocked on the door and woke him from his deep slumber on a sofa.

"Who's that?" he asked.

"Wake up. It's your fairly godmother," I called out.

"Oh, it's just you." He traipsed over, opened the door and went back to the sofa.

"How did you get in without a key?" I asked.

"I jimmied the door with my credit card." He curled up and closed his eyes.

"Too bad they don't have steroids here along with the painkillers and vitamins." I hustled into the training room and turned on the whirlpool. "Then I wouldn't have to score our shit from Simon."

Barrie opened his eyes and sat up. "I can't get back to sleep. I guess I'm up for the day. Let's get into the whirlpool."

"Simon doesn't need the income, either," I said as we went over to the whirlpool.

"Wouldn't it be nice," Barrie said, "if juice was legalized and we could get it here, from the trainers, at no cost?"

"If juice was legalized, everybody in the league would be doing it."

Barrie laughed. "Everybody already *is* doing it. Or at least everybody who wants to do it. Vlad, Pavel and a few others still won't."

We climbed into the bubbling water. "Barrie, tell me about last night."

"Last night was unreal."

"You always say that."

"Well, this time I mean it."

Not long ago, in training camp, Barrie and I sometimes got a room at a hotel close to where we worked out. After our first preseason game, which had been long and difficult, we slipped out after bed check, picked up two girls and took them to our favorite room at the hotel. I felt exhausted, but I also felt very horny.

In the hotel room, my new young lady friend went down on me till I thought my cock would explode. Then I rolled over and fell asleep. I woke up at some point, feeling the bed rock and fearing the huge earthquake we had all dreaded. But no; Barrie created the rocking motion simply by ramming his rod into the girl I had just fucked. Seeing me awake, he leaned over to speak to me.

'Just roll over and pretend nothing's going on,' he said. 'Just go back to sleep.'

So I did. Just another night hanging out with Barrie Weston.

"Unreal," he said now, remembering what he had done while I had gone to the Igloo with Laurel and the others. "Outrageous."

When he got started talking about his sexual conquests, I often just tuned him out and he didn't seem offended. He already had the only audience he really needed: himself.

"Totally beyond human comprehension," he added with a huge sigh. "I must be a hell of a man."

I got out of the whirpool, went past the equipment manager's cage and turned on his boombox. I put on some easy listening music, then grabbed two bottles of Diefenbaker's from the trainer's fridge and returned to the whirlpool.

"There's more where these came from," I said, handing one of the bottles to Barrie. "I know we're not supposed to drink these, but fuck them."

We drank in silence. The beer, though ice cold, did not refresh me. I wanted something sweet, like chocolate milk.

"Why do we deserve to live so well?" Barrie asked as he guzzled the beer. A news junkie, he listened to the myriad stories of people newly unemployed or homeless, and periodically he sank into a funk about the plight of the downtrodden. Fortunately, his empathy and compassion for the have-nots seldom prevented him from enjoying the privileges of being a have.

"Tell me about last night," I said again. He and I had a very strange friendship, indeed, but ours had become my longest and most stable relationship, and for that I felt profoundly grateful.

"Unreal and spectacular," Barrie said, shaking his head.

"Details, please."

"Have you ever met Derry Byrnes?" He looked at me, ready to talk. "He owns Big Sloppy's."

"I've eaten there."

"I talked to his kids last night." Derry Byrnes led one of Bayporte's many youth organizations. "I was just feeling really honest about things."

"Yikes."

Barrie grinned. "So he gave me this really nice introduction and I said what was on my mind. I told these boys that hockey was just fun and entertainment, nothing to take too seriously."

I laughed. "I'm sure Derry wasn't expecting that."

"He didn't like it, but what the fuck? I'm a star and can say whatever I please. As soon as I finished, he jumped up and reminded the kids that hockey and competition and what-not built lifelong friendships, discipline and character."

"I'm sure he won't ask you to speak again."

"So then he says, 'Why don't you come over to my place and have a drink?' I said yes. At his place, I meet his wife. He says, 'Do you like her? Do you want to fuck her? Why don't you call your pal Chris Cross and have him come over? He can fuck her, too.'"

"Bullshit."

"I'm not lying. But I know you don't go in for kink, so I didn't want to invite you to do something that would make you uncomfortable or offend your sensibilities."

"How old was his wife?" I asked.

"Getting up there. She must have been close to forty."

"A real senior citizen, eh?"

"Like I said, it was surreal. I had this boner that wouldn't go down. He stood at the side with a Camcorder. He gave us directions like he was making a porno movie. I went down on her till she nearly screamed."

"All he did was watch? Really?"

Barrie shrugged. "With some guys, that's how they get off. Some guys just want to video record you balling their wives, then they watch it while they jerk off. Everybody's different, I guess."

I nodded. "Tell me more."

"After hours of boffing, we took a shower and she got out these sex toys—"

"Dildoes, vibrators, handcuffs, that sort of thing?"

"Yeah. Just shut up and let me tell the story, OK?"

I smiled and nodded.

"Some of her sex toys looked very menacing, and she had a whole collection of them. Phony cocks, you know? Some of those things could really hurt."

"So you had a good time," I said.

Barrie looked bemused. "I had an exhausting time. That bitch really wore me out."

"Sounds like you wore her out, too," I said.

He smiled. "Fucking right I did. Like I said, 'Why do I live this way?' I'm getting too old for these freaky women and their way-out scenes."

Tommy Stelfox, our fortysomething clubhouse attendant, came in and said, "Cross, who let you in?"

"Barrie did."

"Who gave you a key, Barrie?" Tommy asked.

"No key. I jimmied the lock."

"Oh, that's bloody nice," he said, shaking his head. "I'm amazed you didn't trip the burglar alarm."

"We won't do it again."

Tommy knew how it felt to be treated as a second-class citizen. The Bullies' players and management wasted enormous amounts of money on stupid things, but Warren Gotch made sure that Tommy's salary amounted to chump change. "He does a job a hundred others could do just as well," Gotcha said, "and if he thinks he can get a better deal elsewhere, he should take it."

"Don't worry about a thing, Tommy," I said. "It will never happen again."

Tommy nodded and walked away, to pick up the countless pieces of athletic apparel that littered the clubhouse. I turned to Barrie and nodded for him to continue with his story.

"In the middle of the night," he told me, "his wife fell asleep, so he and I went into the kitchen to get a drink. He called some guy's wife, and she said she was lonely because her husband was away. Her husband didn't care what she did as long as she was discreet about it." He smirked. "He probably would have bragged to the whole world that his missus was getting it on with Barrie J. Weston."

"It would have been the highlight of his life."

"We went over there and did our thing, but Derry left his Camcorder at home."

"At least you won't end up on YouTube," I said.

Barrie snapped his fingers. "I haven't told you the freaky part yet."

"I think I've heard enough."

He looked hurt. "Don't you want to hear the rest? After she'd wounded my Johnson, she left the room. She came back with a syringe. Do you know what she had? A speedball!"

My mouth dropped open. "Speedball?"

He nodded. "A speedball. Heroin and cocaine. Bad stuff, man."

I nodded. "Amen to that."

The door flew open Duncan appeared, enraged. "Whoever did it better confess!"

"Barrie did it." I pointed at Weston.

"I probably did," Barrie said. "What did I do?"

"Someone went into the fridge and took a couple of Diefenbaker's! They're not for players. If you get thirsty, there's a pop machine down the hall."

"The pop costs two bucks each and I never carry any loonies or toonies," I said.

"Then use the water fountain next to the pop machine." He shook his head and walked away.

"Fuck you, too, Duncan," I muttered.

"So," Barrie said as we continued to soak in the whirlpool, "tell me about *your* night."

"Mine?"

"Yes, yours. What did you do for fun last night?"

"I went to Simon's and got down deep into my soul. It's a dangerous place, my soul. He asked about you."

"He knows how I'm doing. He watches hockey. He *knows,* period." Barrie always spoke succinctly and secretively about juicing, as if discussing counterfeiting greenbacks or producing kiddie porn.

"He says the next generation of juice will be along soon," I said.

"The current generation is good enough for me."

"You're not afraid of a piss test, are you?" I asked him.

He looked at me. "Why? Have you heard anything?"

"No, but Jacques and I had that little visit, and if he knew—"

"Then let's make sure he doesn't find out." Barrie paused. "Most of the damn team is doing it, thanks to Wallace Christopher Crossley."

"And the venerable Doctor Simon Kwan turned *me* on and supplies the whole team. He's the reason we're in first place."

We both stayed quiet for a few moments. "So," Barrie finally said, "tell me about last night."

"I went to the Igloo afterwards. Bourdin and Pilon really mixed it up."

Barrie arched an eyebrow. "Did they fight each other?"

"No, but they fought everyone else. One of them did a striptease on stage while the other one pushed away the bouncers. Then they started hitting their girlfriends. When the violence started, I took off with Paterson's date and drove her home."

"Let's hear it for Badass Crossley," Barrie said with a touch of contempt. He remembered our game against the Maple Leafs in Toronto. The fans kept pelting us with debris. Ignas and Weston climbed into the stands and, quickly followed by most other Bullies, started thrashing the troublemakers. Even Jacques got into the melee, grabbing at the arms of some kid trying to strangle Mark Ignas. The TV cameras covered the entire brawl, naturally, including the Bullies' bench, which held one occupant, the one man who refused to fight: Christopher Crossley.

"You think they got busted at the Igloo last night because of that fighting?" I asked Barrie.

"No, they're Bullies. The cops love them and would ask for autographs."

Then Harv Arthur, our fast-rising second-line forward, came in and got into the water with us.

"Hey, guys," he said. "So hot in here. How do you stand it?"

"Some like it hot," Barrie said.

"I am totally exhausted," Harv said. "The kid was crying all night. Little bugger just wouldn't shut up. How you doing, Barrie?"

Harv, a three-sport standout at Notre Dame, hoped that soon Jacques would promote him to first line and bust Barrie down to second line. Harv did everything nearly as well as Barrie did. He just needed some experience.

"Did you hear about Pilon and Bourdin at the Igloo last night?" Harv asked.

"Yes," I answered. "Bourdin was wagging his weenie again in public."

Harv shook his head. "Crazy bunch of guys here." He didn't go to the Igloo or stick needles in his wazoo. He invested in Bayporte real estate. After retiring, he would buy the rest of Canada.

"That'll be the last time for those guys, making fools of themselves in public." Harv said.

"Wrong," Barrie said. "Donny likes getting naked in front of people. That's what turns him on."

"Are you keeping busy in real estate right now, Harv?" I asked.

He shrugged. "Got a few things going with some people out in the Valley. Good thing I have a smart phone. That's how I visit the office to see how we're doing."

"So you have two careers going on at the same time," Barrie said.

"How are old buggers like Cross and me supposed to keep up with you kids?"

We left the whirlpool and heard *bhangra* music in the hallway. Jacques always insisted that the cage person play popular songs by Canadian artists; he would go ballistic over that cornball Indian hip-hop music. He could throw as spectacular a temper tantrum as anyone I had ever met, especially over trivial things like hearing the wrong music on the sound system.

I toweled off and wandered into the lobby. Mark Ignas stood at the glass-enclosed, locked bulletin board, sliding off the little chrome lock that, to my knowledge, had never actually been snapped shut. He tacked a message on the board, closed the little glass door and slid the lock back into place.

"Check it out," he said as he walked away.

ALL PLAYERS SHOULD HAVE THE RIGHT TO USE PERFORMANCE-ENHANCING DRUGS IF THEY CHOOSE TO DO SO.

Barrie came along, as naked as myself, and pointed at the message. "Who put *that* shit up there?"

"Mark Ignas, just now."

"Are you sure it wasn't Wally Horton?"

"Horton's too dumb to write something like that. The message makes sense."

"Yeah, I like it. Steroids are good for you. They pump up the love muscle." Barrie dropped his towel and grabbed his penis, simulating masturbation.

"They'll probably think *I* put up that message. I'm the kind to pull a stunt like that."

"Poor little man," Barrie said, looking at his member. "Got to give you a few days off."

We walked back to the locker room.

"Have you ever been in love?" I asked him.

"I was married."

"Yeah, but have you ever been in love?"

Barrie smiled, appreciating my retort.

"How about any of your girlfriends?" I asked. "Were you in love with them?"

"The girl who took my virginity," Barrie said. "Can't remember her name, but I had deep feelings for her when we were together. She made a man of me, I think. That's as close as I have ever come to being in love. How about you?"

"I've never been in love, either. I'm starting to think that love just doesn't exist." I looked in my locker and opened a few pieces of mail I had neglected, mainly because the correspondence that ended up in my locker deserved my neglect. The credit card companies always sent me preapproved applications and the local charities always hit me up for donations, as if I hadn't already given enough money to worthy causes.

One letter looked as if a child had written it. I didn't know how to respond to a child's letter, since I had been a child once myself and hated to break their little hearts.

The letter said:

Hi Chris Cross

You are the bestest playr and the Bullys are the bestest team. I hope you get in the hall of Fame but my Dad sez your not good enuf.

Your frend an fan,

Cliffy Waselowich

P.S. Do you know Barrie Weston could you please get him to send me his ottografed picture? Thanks

I felt like writing on the bottom of his note, *You should learn to write before you worry about autographed pictures* and sending it back to him. Instead, I slipped it into Barrie's locker.

In the training room, I moaned and groaned on the table as Duncan worked on me to maximize my flexibility.

"Hey, Cross," said Donny Bourdin, entering the room. "Does that poking and pulling do you any good?"

"I pretend that it does," I answered. I did enjoy the rubdowns.

Donny had distinguished himself as one of the NHL's men-to-watch list. Early on, Jacques and Gotcha had threatened to trade him because of his "poor attitude and lack of team spirit." In other words, Donny's agent demanded more money than Gotcha wanted to pay.

Sometime last year, Jacques benched Bourdin and put in Joe Rossi, a top draft pick from Toronto. After a brief losing streak, Jacques suddenly observed "an improved attitude" on the part of the bench-warming Bourdin, put him back in and made Rossi sit.

Jacques said, "Rossi is the best young player in the league," then simply refused to let him play. Confused and heartbroken about why Jacques praised then punished him, Rossi took me aside and implored me to explain the matter to him. I told him the truth: I didn't understand Jacques any better than he did, but I *did* understand that the Bayporte Bullies, the NHL and life in general were all unfair.

Rossi told local sports reporters that he felt frustrated and enraged, and that he wanted to be traded. That evening, Jacques sent him to the Hartford Whalers as a way of discouraging the rest of us from pooh-poohing the Bullies to the media. I met up with Rossi just before he headed out to Connecticut. He seemed like a survivor of 9/11, sighing and shaking his head, not wanting to play for the Whalers and still unable to comprehend why Jacques handled the whole matter so heartlessly. Soon afterwards, Hartford released Rossi and he disappeared from the NHL.

Bourdin, however, had become one of the Bullies' key players, and as I got my rubdown in the training room, he walked past me and headed to the counter, shook out a few vitamin tablets and gobbled them up. Bourdin, barring concussions or chronic orthopedic problems, could someday become a Hall of Fame inductee if he maintained his productivity and didn't get caught juicing.

"Cross," Donny said, "did you catch Bryant Forrester on the radio this morning? He has this contest going where you send an email of about fifty words predicting the highlights of our next game. The email that's most accurate wins four Bullies tickets." He paused. "Denis Pilon's mum entered the contest."

Pilon's mother, a vivacious single woman, moved to Bayporte when her son became a Bully. Mum Pilon would panic if she didn't check in with her boy every day, and he begged her to quit bugging him and let him be his own man.

"I don't know what she said in her email," Bourdin added, "but it will probably freak him out. She freaks him out very easily."

Denis Pilon and Donny Bourdin were the greatest of friends on a team where most of the players were ambivalent about each other. They practiced together and partied every weekend. Some of the other guys, envious and contemptuous, called Donny and Denis "bum buddies."

Once, I sat listening to a conversation in the steam room. The talk, after going from financial and post-retirement issues, settled for a few minutes on interracial relationships. Mark Ignas, our only non-Caucasian teammate, once asked Lucy Rybka to dance at a Bullies' party. Vlad, Lucy's husband, promised to rearrange Mark's handsome Native face if Ignas ever did that again.

"That punk redskin," the big Russian remembered, indignant. "You know what he did? He said to her, 'Wanna dance?'"

"Shame on him," I said.

"Focking right," said Vlad. "They should send that redskin focker back to whatever country he come from."

"Vlad," I explained, a bit embarrassed for him, "Ignas is a Native North American. He comes from *here*. That's why they call him a Native. Are you retarded?"

I didn't feel Vlad's fist as it smashed into the back of my head. I did feel myself tumbling around and trying to stop the white pain as it flashed through my brain. I stopped and sat for a moment or so until the excruciating sensations faded a bit. Then I lunged at Vlad, who simply pushed me away, right through the doorway and out into the hallway. I groped my way back to my locker and vomited all over myself. I felt queasy for the next few days and vowed to shut the fuck up around Vlad and all other big crazy Russians.

I lay on the training table and Duncan told me to turn over.

Bourdin, who had been crunching away on vitamin tablets, walked to the head of the table and began pumping his crotch into my face.

"Ooh baby baby," he said.

I kept my mouth closed.

"Open wide, baby," he said.

"Baby don't want it," I said.

"But Daddy wants it," Bourdin said.

"Donny," Duncan interjected, "if you don't have any legitimate business being here, take off."

"I'm just trying to git me some," Bourdin said.

"You don't know where's his mouth been, Bourdin," Barrie said as he entered the room. "Cross is the biggest slut in town. You can get some nasty diseases from him."

"Listen to him, Donny," I said. "That man speaks the truth."

Barrie sat down naked on the table, his bare bum just inches from my face. Even though the sign said that all players must wear jockstraps and T-shirts, Barrie walked around butt-naked with total impunity, for some reason.

"Donny," Barrie asked, "why are you trying to stick your dick down his throat? What about Barbara?"

Donny looked sad. "Barbara won't eat my meat. She thinks it's unhygienic and morally depraved."

"Then get some head from the groupies."

"I would, but I don't like cheating on my sweetie."

Just then, Barrie ripped a huge fart.

"Get your ass off this table!" Duncan and I yelled. Barrie did as told.

Donny laughed and waved his hand. "Whoa!" He left the room.

Harv came in, dressed in a jockstrap and T-shirt. He came up behind Barrie and slid his arms around Barrie's waist. He kissed Barrie's shoulder, and Barrie caressed Harv's long, muscular arms.

"This young fellow," said Barrie, speaking of Harv, "may make it into the Hall of Fame one day. But I'll tell you this: he'll never be able to party worth shit."

Harv hung his head and pretended to cry. "I know. I'm such a wimp."

"If you teach Barrie how to trip another player and get away with it," I said to Harv, "he'll teach you how to drink an entire bottle of Canadian Comfort without puking."

Barrie and Harv frowned at each other, then laughed at my joke. The three of us left the training room and went into the sauna.

"You know that message someone tacked up on the bulletin board?" Barrie asked us as we sat in the oppressive heat.

Harv, a non-juicer, shook his head, largely clueless of that part of Bullies life. He might go to the bosses if he knew about our pills and needles. We had to speak carefully around him.

"I read it," Harv said, snarling as if someone had pasted Nazi propaganda on his front door. "It advocated the use of performance-enhancing drugs."

"Well," Barrie said, "Jacques took it down."

"I'm sure he'll say something about it in the next meeting," I said.

Donny Bourdin poked his head in and yelled, "I hate you people!"

"You sure liked *me* a few minutes ago!" I hollered back.

"Jacques doesn't think steroids are anything to laugh about," Harv said.

"Jacques has no sense of humor," I muttered.

Barrie shook his head and mouthed, *Shut up.*

I nodded and stood up. "Well, gentlemen, *I* didn't put that bit of wisdom up there on the bulletin board, so it's not my problem."

Barrie shrugged. "I don't know anything, I just work here."

Soon Duncan McCallum barged in. "All right! Who did it?"

"Did what?" I asked.

"Who drank my beer?" McCallum yelled. "Don't tell me you didn't."

"I'm innocent, I tell you! I didn't do anything wrong!"

"Yeah, I'll bet," McCallum said.

Trainers, every team's unsung heroes, had the impossible job of being accountable for the health of each player. The team's bosses placed little confidence in them because the trainers were not physicians. Roderick, Jacques and Warren cared very little about the players; they wanted to win games and make money. Trainers, like car mechanics, taped or lubed whatever broke down until the damage became irreparable.

'Anything else I can do for you?' McCallum once asked me after a rubdown.

'Yeah,' I said. 'Make me a Stanley Cup ring.'

'No can do. Want some vitamins? A B-12 shot?'

'That's very tempting, but no.' I headed back into the locker room and dozed off in the aging recliner we kept in the corner. I dreamed of pills and liquids I wasn't supposed to have, drugs that did me a hell of a lot more good than Duncan McCallum's rubdowns, vitamins and B-12 injections.

I called Monique and made plans to meet up with her back east. She would fly out there with Thornton and our team. I continued speaking to her on my iPhone until Gish shouted that our meeting would start in two minutes. I said goodbye to Monique, tossed the phone into my locker, changed into my sweatsuit and hurried into the meeting room.

Barrie motioned for me to sit next to him and I answered when Gish called my name. Gish glowered at me, then stepped back as Jacques stepped forward. Jacques held Ignas' message from the bulletin board.

"He thinks you put it up there," Barrie muttered.

"Did someone speak?" Jacques asked. He got mad whenever someone spoke in a meeting without receiving permission to do so.

"I was just clearing my throat," I said.

"Oh? I definitely heard speech. I believe we would all enjoy hearing what you just said, Crossley."

"Sir, I didn't say anything."

Jacques, his face twisted in disgust, held Ignas' message some distance from his body, its white corner pinched between his right thumb and forefinger, as if displaying someone's bloodied Tampax.

"I'm sure we have all seen *this* bit of business by now. Clearly, there seems to be a player among us who believes that it is OK not to play by the rules."

The harshness of Jacques' tone terrified me. He had gotten rid of players who had expressed controversial opinions or used the bulletin board to publicize their own views. Ignas had been a damn fool to tack that message up there.

"...anyone who thinks 'I' comes before 'us'..."

My face reddened. My stomach boiled. Still, I knew the guilty party; if necessary, I would snitch on him.

"...we have no use for troublemakers here..."

No use. Jacques meant it. After all, he'd had no use for Garrett Tannenbaum.

Tannenbaum's demotion to the minors reminded us of one of Jacques' more curious idiosyncrasies. In a meaningless game against the Sharks, with only a minute on the clock, we had possession of the puck and were down 2-1. We were on a power play, with a one-man advantage. Weston passed the puck to Tannenbaum; the Sharks' goalie, momentarily disoriented, turned each way, unable to locate the puck, which was on Tannenbaum's stick, two feet from the net. Tannenbaum had an effortless shot into a half-empty net, but nerves overcame him and he got off the feeblest of shots that ricocheted off the goalie. A Shark got the puck, passed it to a teammate, who moments later swept the puck past Mike Fillo.

In his postgame remarks, Jacques spoke mainly about Tannenbaum's poor shot on goal and implied that Tannenbaum had singlehandedly cost us the game. Nobody dared to suggest that Jacques was being a bit too hard on Garrett. For months afterwards, in the training room, we watched footage of Tannenbaum's bad play, in slow motion, frozen and from every possible angle.

We had *no use* for Tannenbaum. *No use* at all.

"We will soon play in the postseason for the first time," Jacques said now, still holding Ignas' message. "Gentlemen, I am not by nature a political man. Whenever I have a problem, I can usually find the answers I need within myself. However, I am concerned, as I believe you are, about the trouble that is defiling our world. Crack cocaine, prostitution, disrespect, random violence. Some believe it is the work of international terrorist organizations. I do not claim to have all the answers, but when I see something like this bit of stupidity on our bulletin board, I begin to wonder if we are all on the same team, so to speak. The player who wrote this should man up and explain himself to the team."

"Jacques..." My voice sounded loud but not altogether confident. I looked up and down, from side to side, then finally at him.

He looked at me, as if surprised but subtly pleased by my decision to "man up" and confess. His face relaxed a bit and he seemed ready to let me stand and speak. I would ask everyone's forgiveness; he would forgive me on everyone's behalf. I would promise to stop putting messages on the board, and we would pretend that the incident had never happened.

"Jacques," I continued, "I'm not sure why you are so offended. I read that thing, too, and it was just one man's opinion. I'm not sure what angered you about it."

"It did anger me, and I just explained why," Jacques said, his blue eyes icy.

"Well, I'm not trying to offend you or anyone else," I said. "But when I read that message, I wasn't offended."

Jacques stared at me. He would get no confession today, from me or anyone else.

He wanted to extract a confession from me and trade me to another team. He couldn't have cared less about me or anyone else. To him, his players were just numbers and statistics. Maybe Barrie Weston was the exception. Jacques tried to stay on amicable terms with Barrie, so Jacques would probably just let the matter drop.

"Let's take a break," he said.

I let out a huge sigh. He wouldn't be sending me to Phoenix or St. Louis today.

Denis Pilon bolted from the training room and headed for his locker to get his cell phone. He needed to call his mother and find out more about her email to Bryant Forrester. Some of us of us went over to the equipment manager's cage to sign pucks.

Barrie reached into the bottomless pile of pucks, picked one up, grabbed a grease pencil and scribbled his name. We had agreed to sign a certain number of pucks each season for sale on the team's Website and gift shop; Barrie also had a side deal to sell autographed pucks on eBay. Barrie bragged often that only Gretzky and Bobby Orr sold more online signed pucks than he did.

"The cops called Jacques last night about what happened at the Igloo," Donny Bourdin said as he did his autographs. "He called us, and he sounded pretty mad about it, but he didn't actually threaten to do anything to us." He looked at me. "You took off with Paterson's girl, hey?"

"Yeah," I muttered, frowning as I struggled to fit my signature on the small black round surface of the puck.

"Paterson was really angry, you know," Donny said. "He threw a temper tantrum. He said you were trying to make time with his best girl."

"He doesn't own her, OK?"

"Well, I just don't like to see a nice guy like him get shitted on."

"He's a bloody goof," I said. As a public man, I had met far too many people who thought they were my friends because they had shaken my hand or posed for a cell phone picture with me. I really got freaked out when parasites like Paterson infiltrated my social circle for the purposes of getting me to invest with him so he could make money off me. Had he actually thrown a temper tantrum over Laurel and me at the Igloo? If she had no interest in him, couldn't he simply buy himself a new girlfriend? Maybe, I thought, this guy needed to go back to Peaceful Village for a while and chill out.

We were fine-tuning our power play when the inevitable fight started. Vlad, a defenseman, stood in the crease, directly in front of Mike Fillo, our first-string goalie. Next to Vlad stood Wally Horton, whose job involved somehow getting Vlad away from Fillo, and Vlad needed to get Horton away from Fillo, or at least make sure that Horton didn't get to the puck and flip it in past Fillo. Horton had speed but Vlad had size; Horton, unable to shove Vlad away from the net, Horton tied him up with his legs and stick. Soon, the two men appeared to be square dancing in front of the exasperated goalie.

"Dammit, Vlad!" yelled Jimmie Gish at the big, frustrated Russian. "Are you going to let Horton make a fool of you in front of everyone? Maybe we should let him have your job and you can just sit on the bench."

Vlad stood there, nodding, hangdog. The power play consisted of Barrie, myself and Mark Ignas. We had the greatest fun, passing the puck back and forth. Ignas took a slap shot that hit Vlad on the leg. Horton sneaked around him, got control of the rebound and swept it past a diving Fillo.

"Vlad," Gish called out, his voice laden with sarcasm, "if you don't think you can cut it out there, just say so."

Vlad scraped his stick into the ice the way he usually did whenever he wanted to thrust it up someone's rectum.

When Gish blew the whistle for the power play to begin, Barrie passed the puck to me and Vlad speared Horton with his stick, and the fight began. Both big men flung off their gloves and started pounding away at each other, sounding as violently guttural as football linemen right after the snap. Fillo slid away as they kept pummeling each other like beasts in the wild.

Gish and Jacques watched, probably smiling at this display of two big men trying to maim each other.

Soon Gish skated towards the two combatants, holding up his hands. "All right, that's enough." Vlad pushed him in the chest so hard that he went sprawling backwards and fell on his ass. Everyone laughed and hooted.

Vlad tore off his helmet and threw punches at Horton, who deftly ducked and kicked Vlad with the blade of his skate. A big red slash appeared through the part of Vlad's socks covering his shin. Vlad picked up his helmet and threw it at Horton, who ducked. The helmet hit Pavel Pavlovich in the face.

"Vlad, you focking moron! Hit him, not me!" Pavel then lunged at Vlad. The two Russians began a wrestling match in front of the vacant net. Gish, now back on his feet, tried to prevent Horton from stick-whipping Vlad, who for the moment could not defend himself.

"Wally," Gish said, "cool down. You've had you fun for the day."

Horton sneered at Gish and tried to maneuver around the coach. "Get out of my way, shit-for-brains!"

Gish, a big man now flabby, weak and old, shook his head and refused to go away. Most of the team, amused by Gish's attempts at being tough, stood around the two fighters and befuddled coach. Pavel sat on Vlad's chest, the two of them swearing at each other, while Gish stood in front of Wally Horton, his hands on Horton's stomach.

"Get your hands off me before I pound you," Horton said to Gish.

"Take it easy, Wally—"

Just then, Horton grabbed Gish by the shirt and shook him like a rag doll. Gish tore himself away and skated off to the safety of the penalty box as we all doubled over with laughter. Gish pushed past Jacques and hustled into the clubhouse. Jacques told us to go take a shower, and we all did so, laughing and shaking our heads at our disgraced coach.

I felt good and decided to forget about rubdowns and whatever else the trainers insisted I needed. I would just do my own thing, my own way.

"Want to join us for a beer?" Barrie asked. "I thought I would start corrupting Harv a bit more."

"Maybe next time. I have some porn downloads I want to check out."

"OK," Barrie said, nodding. "Show yourself a nice time."

That afternoon, I drove through the east Bayporte slum on my way to Laurel's house.

The Bayporte Natives, Canada's most oppressed people, live just a few minutes from the sparkling affluence of downtown, but they scarcely even pretend to strive for better lives. Better lives? Better than whose? The whites rarely give the Natives more than lip service. The Natives watch and say nothing, knowing they will always be last and least.

I pulled into a full-service gas station and an older Indian man with a turban approached me.

"May I help you?" he asked.

"Fill 'er with the regular," I said. He looked at me for several moments before going to the rear of my car and unscrewing my gas cap.

Then he came back to me and studied my face some more. I gave him my American Express card and he beamed. "Yes! I know you! How are you, Chris Cross!" He extended his hand for me to shake.

"Surviving," I told him, flattered by his delight in meeting me.

"I have been watching you play ever since I moved to Bayporte."

"That long, eh?"

His face fell. "I want to ask you: can you do something about the big new stadium they are going to build soon? It will be very bad for my business. Very bad." He shook his head and sighed.

He pointed to another Indian man behind the counter of the minimart. "My partner and I and a couple of other men have been going to your hockey games for a long time now. We are having just enough money for four tickets at center ice and a tank of gas. If they build that new stadium, there will be higher ticket prices and we will not be having the money to go."

"I can't help you with that," I replied. "I'm just hired help. They don't ask me, 'Cross, is it OK for us to build a big new stadium?'"

"When I first came to Bayporte, I could easily afford these hockey tickets and many other things, even rock concerts. I am making more money now but somehow can afford fewer things," the man explained.

"I think it's called inflation and economics," I said. "Makes you feel like a drug addict. They give you the drugs for free till you become addicted, then they charge you top dollar because you can't live without it."

He looked at me with big, wrinkled brown eyes. "You have spoken the truth. I don't know we will find the money for hockey games now. Are you sure there is nothing you can do about this bad situation?"

I crossed my fists at him, as if I were wearing handcuffs.

The gas stopped flowing and the man took my credit card. He waved to the man inside, who came out and had a look at my credit card. He stuck his hand into my window and shook my hand.

"Nice to meet you, Chris Cross!" he said.

"Mutual," I said.

"Will you be playing in the new stadium?" he asked.

"I'll do whatever my bosses tell me to do."

"It is too bad, that these things happen," he said.

They returned my credit card, we shook hands again and I drove off.

Soon I left Bayporte and headed into the Tyson Valley. I always loved escaping the huge city and going to the mountains, hills and wildlife that stretched for miles. I saw the cattle grazing and the birds flying, the pace of life slowed down and appreciated. The sky was clear, the wind fresh.

Lately the trip to the Valley had taken longer as more city people, with big-money jobs in the Financial District, moved there because of the wide-open spaces and irresistible housing prices. For the price of a decent-sized downtown Bayporte condominium, a person could buy a three-bedroom home and have a front lawn the size of a football field. But plenty of available land remained in the Valley, accessible and beautiful, and at times I believed that my fantasy of settling out there, among the huge trees, hills and wildlife, kept me from going bonkers in Bayporte. But moving out here? My only skills were playing hockey, shooting steroids and screwing girls. What would I do in the Valley?

I waved at the sign saying WELCOME TO WHITLEY. Just beyond, at a convenience store's parking lot, three or four local guys stood by a truck, all of them wearing mackinaws, faded Levi's and beanies. Those Valley boys pointed at me and whispered to each other. While they decided whether or not to come over, say hi and admire my BMW, I sped away from them.

I reached Laurel's home and immediately saw a silver Cadillac parked in the driveway. I recognized it as Pat Paterson's car. He stood at the front door, confronting Jaspal Singh.

"Don't give me any backtalk. Just let me in," Paterson said, his red face blending well with his blue Brioni suit and burgundy tie. Gleaming black shoes completed the look.

"Laurel says she doesn't want you coming by again," Jaspal said, his face taut with rage. He crossed his arms and stood his ground.

I walked over to Paterson's car and leaned on it. He and Jaspal seemed oblivious to my presence.

"Unreal," Paterson said, sighing. "A bloody Punjab won't let me in to see my own girlfriend." He looked around, as if expecting backups to materialize from somewhere to help him get past Jaspal.

"Just get back into your car and go away, all right?" Jaspal paused. "This is a nice peaceful place. Let's keep it that way."

"If you want to keep the peace, just let me go in and see Laurel."

Just then Jaspal grabbed Paterson by the tie and pulled him so close that their chins were nearly touching. "Listen, fatso, do you want me to pound you?"

Paterson threw up his hands in surrender. "Don't have get violent, you know."

"I'll kick your ass all over the Valley if you call me any more names. Now bugger off before I start to get rude." Jaspal let go of his tie, then pushed Paterson backwards. Pat nearly fell but gathered himself together and smoothed out his tie. "I blame you for all this," he said to me. The back of his elegant Brioni suit coast bore a huge oval sweat stain. "You ran off with Laurel at the Igloo. Everyone laughed at me. Is that how you treat your friends?"

"Paterson," I replied, "you don't have any friends. You never have and never will. Now get out of here."

He skulked over to his big gleaming car, started it up and drove up to me. "Hockey hotshot. Big fucking deal!" he shouted. "Hockey homo! Faggot!" Then he drove off.

"What an asshole," I said.

"I hope he doesn't come back," Jaspal said as the Cadillac disappeared into the distance.

"I meet people like him all the time. They need to get a life." Then, "Is Laurel around?"

"Yes," he said. "She's out in the back, castrating some calves. She'll be glad to see you."

"Castrating calves, eh? I think I'll wait for her in here."

The moon sat huge and low on the horizon and we reclined on Laurel's patio, staring in awe of the vastness of the Valley sky. The evening, a bit on the warm side, felt just about perfect for me, but my confrontation with Paterson troubled me. Laurel and I had eaten a big dinner of barbecued steaks, and our filthy plates and glasses were stacked to the side.

"I'm glad you didn't mind my driving out here uninvited," I said.

She smiled. "I hate having dinner alone."

She had barbecued the steaks while Jaspal and I smoked pot and talked about sports. I got the impression that he really wanted me to tell him about all the juicing felt sure the Bullies had done. As soon as we finished eating, Jaspal went back to finish his work.

Weird sounds filled the air: birds, dogs and other animals from miles away. Car doors opened and closed; vehicles sped by. I swore I heard gunshots but then decided I didn't.

Laurel and I squirmed and shifted.

"Are you uncomfortable?" she asked.

"No, just the opposite," I said. I looked up. "I sure love this great big Valley sky. It's so much different from Bayporte, somehow."

She smirked. "In Bayporte, the smog and skyscrapers block your view of everything that's worth seeing."

We fell silent for a few minutes and listened to night sounds. We also heard the *thunk* of a car's trunk closing and some kids shouting above each other.

"Hear those voices?" Laurel asked. "Those are my neighbors. They're so far away, but their voices carry. I love those rural acoustics."

I nodded. The sky, so full of sparkling stars and the smells of nature, made me want to laugh at the poor, deluded Bayporters who spent most of their time and energy making money, getting laid and buying the most expensive status symbols they could find. As I sat out here in the Valley, I thought city people's priorities seemed ludicrous.

"So beautiful here," I murmured to Laurel. "You're so beautiful. Let's go inside and spend the night together."

"Mozart, right?" I asked, spread-eagled across Laurel's bed as beautiful music floated in from another room. "Mostly, I don't know jackshit about classical music, but I know that one."

"Very good," she said. "Have you seen *Amadeus*?"

She rolled over on me. I lay face down and could feel her hot breath on my neck and her body's warmth all over me. She kissed me between my shoulder blades.

"Beautiful movie," she said. "I have it on DVD. Want to see it?"

"Not right now."

We made long, soft, tender love to each other. We kept our eyes closed and enjoyed this experience through our other senses. I mounted her and pressed into her. I pumped for the longest time.

"Oh," she said. "Unh." She arched her back and threw back her head. Afterwards, we lay together, and I felt desperately unhappy, more apart than ever from the world.

"I want to tell you something." I sat up in bed as Laurel lay alongside me. "I don't know if I'm happy, and I've always thought that the goal of life was *knowing* I was happy."

She shook her head. "Happiness is the satisfaction you get from living well. You don't say, 'I want to be happy,' you say, 'I want to do those things that will make me happy.'"

"I didn't know that."

"Happiness comes from having someone to love. You can make each other happy. When they're happy, so are you."

"How can you tell when you're happy and they're happy?" I asked.

"You just *can*."

I pondered her words for a bit. "I'm happy when I score a goal. I'm happy when the crowd cheers me on and Jacques doesn't rag on me. I guess that's about it."

"Oh, and don't I make you happy?" she asked, her eyes narrowing.

"You're in my bed, we've just had sex, and now you're saying that only hockey makes you happy. Hockey and a bunch of drunken assholes whistling and hollering your name. No wonder you're unhappy most of the time."

"Sorry," I muttered. "I didn't mean it that way. Shit, I probably try to make myself unhappy. You've given me the only pleasure I've had lately."

"So you like being here?"

"I *love* being here. Right now, I'm dreading the drive back to Bayporte and the flight back east. I'd like to spend the rest of my life right here with you, in this bed."

"If you moved in with me—"

"I would be a happy fucking man." I leaned over and kissed her. "I can't play hockey forever, and we're the team on everyone's shit list because they think we're juicers. If I fail one piss test, it's goodbye, Chris Cross."

"So maybe you better start planning for life after hockey."

"If I moved in with you, what could I do?"

"Oh," she said, "there's plenty you could do. Right now, this place isn't much more than a house with a huge back yard and some cows. We could turn it into a big, efficient ranch and you could be the boss."

"Wow! Sounds like a big deal."

She shook her head. "Or maybe not. You don't have to do it. Anyway, it would be better for you than being an NHL Bully. I think you know that, and maybe you're ready for a major change of lifestyle."

I nodded. "Tell me more."

"If you got sick of doing the work, you could just sort of be the man of the house. I have plenty of money. We could just concentrate on learning to live with less."

"Less of what?" I asked.

"Less of all that stuff that makes us miserable. Most people are taught all their lives to accumulate shiny new toys, and those shiny toys get in our way and make it impossible for us to see each other, know each other and accept each other. We could start out with having too much and get rid of it until ultimately those shiny toys are gone and it's just you and me and there's nothing between us except air. That would be our life's goal in this chaotic, cluttered universe."

"So we'd start with everything and end up with nothing?"

"We'd start with everything that didn't matter and end up with nothing except what did matter. And if either of us said, 'Wait! I can't do this,' the dissatisfied one would just walk away."

I put my arms around her and said, "I think this is the start of a beautiful relationship."

She smiled. "Let's do it."

5

The morning breeze felt fresh as I sauntered over to my car. The sun was gentle but warm on my neck as I got into my car and crept towards the front gate. Laurel looked angelic on her front porch, waving and beaming, as if beckoning me to forget about my meaningless life and run back into her arms. A part of me wanted to do just that, to leave my car halfway on the roadway and spend the rest of my life making love to Laurel and having many beautiful children with her. But I had business to do with Barrie Weston, Jacques, Warren Gotch, Roderick Rainey and myself. Then I would return to Laurel and never leave her.

As I drove away, I saw a brown hand waving and heard the

words, "Break a leg!"

What an odd bit of advice to give a hockey player, I thought. But Jaspal meant well. I honked and waved back.

Then I got onto the road and drove towards the metropolis the national magazines called "Canada's Finest City."

At Bayporte International Airport, reporters and fans had packed into our departure area. We, the players, sat isolated in the V.I.P. lounge, where smiling cuties in Canadian Airways uniforms brought us coffee and pop.

Before reaching the airport, I had gone home to get a change of clothes and my MacBook computer. In the lounge, I put my computer at my feet and checked out the other faces. Harv Arthur sat forlorn in a corner, his chin nearly reaching his chest and a Bullies cap pulled well over his eyes.

I went over and tapped his shoulder. "Harv, you OK?"

"Go away," he muttered.

"Harv, it's me, Cross."

"What you want?" He pushed back his cap and looked up at me, his eyes terribly bloodshot and his face in need of a shave.

"Harv, are you sick?" I asked.

"Too much booze," he managed to say, licking his chapped lips. "Too much fun. Too much Barrie Weston."

"Did you two pick up any women?"

He let out a tiny, weak laugh. "I got bitten and scratched. She screamed at me. She wanted me to bite her, too."

"Glad I missed that."

"I had to tell my wife a bunch of lies. Not sure if she believed me."

"Where's Barrie?" I asked.

"After we got through with the crazy women at about one, Barrie said we should go to this after-hours jazz club down near skid row. I think I fell asleep in there, and when I woke up, he'd taken off with his car. I had to take a taxi home. Then I came here." He groaned.

"That's too bad, Harv." One of the smiling ladies came by with a tray of drinks and I took a Coke. I got up to stretch my legs and spotted Skylar "Snoop" Kowalski. He came over and asked me to grant him an interview.

Kowalski covered sports for Channel 4's highly popular Website and most of his job involved following the Bullies around. The most incompetent journalist I had ever encountered, Snoop always got falling-down drunk before games. Then he staggered into the press section and looked over the shoulders of the other reporters, to see what he'd missed. Then he would file his own story. Barrie and I had nicknamed him Snoop for that reason.

He had won several awards for excellence in Canadian sports journalism. A spectacular drunk and druggie, Snoop was the life of any party, but knowing him caused me much grief. Sometimes, after an interview with him, I would click on my iPad and find three or four full screens of truths, half-truths and outright lies he had attributed to me.

"Piss off, Snoop," I said to him in the airport lounge. "Just go away and leave me alone."

"In NHL circles, they're saying your whole team is using banned substances," Snoop said into his tiny voice recorder. "Any comment?"

"Snoop—"

"When confronted with the ugly rumors about the drugs, Crossley threatened me with a hockey-stick enema."

"I did not threaten you. I just told you to piss off."

"Yeah, but that's boring. If my readers get boring quotes, they'll stop reading."

"Snoop," I said, "why don't you go pick on somebody your own size?" I had six inches and forty pounds on him.

"Look, Cross, I'm the best friend you've got, even if you don't think so. And remember: All publicity is good publicity. I'm making you into a legend in your own time."

"Charles Manson is a legend in his own time, too. Dammit, Snoop, Jacques is still angry about your story from last month."

He shrugged. "I don't remember it."

"You quoted me as saying that Reg MacKenzie has a face like a pepperoni pizza."

"Well, he *does*."

I harrumphed. "So what? You shouldn't have written such a thing. I don't want to speak to you or give you another interview."

"All right, you don't need to get mad about it. I'm just a guy doing a job. Where's Weston?"

I ignored him and walked away, to board the aircraft.

I smiled as I took my seat, soothed by the sights, sounds and smells of air travel. Flying still gave me a thrill, even after thousands of hours in the air. I could only relax and be myself while other, unseen people worried about how to get me to my destination. If the Taliban were onboard and blew up the plane, c'est la vie.

Weston slept in the seat next to me, smelling very much like the vagrants who populated skid row. Shuffling and mumbling, the last to board the plane, he had collapsed into his seat just before losing consciousness. By some miracle, he would be ready to play, and find a way to win, once we got back on the ice. He had confided to me that he felt truly alive and happy only while playing hockey. Off the ice, he whored around out of boredom and eagerly awaited our next game. Only hockey gave him the thrill he needed.

'But it's the same for you, too, eh?' he had once said. 'We get big money so we can live well and eat well. We're privileged, so maybe we should be grateful for that, while our privileges last.'

I looked at him now: my privileged, hung over superstar teammate, sprawled on the big cushy seat, his eyes closed and mouth open, designer clothes all wrinkled. I sat back and thought for a moment about how happy Laurel English made me.

"Hiya, Cross," said Linda Gee, a Canadian Airways flight attendant, smiling down at me. Last season, after we had won a couple of road games, Linda masturbated Barrie on the flight back to Bayporte.

A fan had sent us some cases of decent wine for the trip home that time, so everyone guzzled it down. Some players received severe reprimands because they drunkenly mouthed off at Roderick Rainey and Warren Gotch. Linda and Barrie were relatively tame and discreet in their naughtiness.

On that memorable flight, Barrie confronted Linda Gee in an isolated part of the plane and requested oral gratification. She told him no, she couldn't do *that*, but she walked him back to his seat, sat down next to him, covered them both with a big blanket and, with both hands, waxed his dolphin while he grunted and groaned. I looked away, envious. Afterwards, she went off to fix dainty snacks for Warren Gotch and the other V.I.P.s.

"Hey, Linda, how goes it?" I asked now.

"I'm depressed," she said. "I have to go out with Thornton Rainey tonight. I don't know why, because he brought his fiancée with him. Maybe they have something kinky in mind."

"Nothing kinky there. He'll go out with you and leave Monique out of it," I said.

"The only reason I agreed to go out with him is that I didn't think I had the option of saying no to him."

"Yeah, you can't turn him down."

She sighed. "I'll make sure I get really drunk."

"It's a shame you won't be free tonight. I wanted to take you somewhere and get something straight between us," I joked. Monique, Thornton's fiancée, invited me to hook up with her at a party given by a New York friend of hers.

"Get us some Winstrol or Deca for the return trip, OK?" I asked Linda.

She nodded. "If I can."

Linda had many contacts, some of whom could provide her with airline-sized bottles of steroids. She said that her bosses at Canadian Airways paid little attention to what she carried on and off the aircraft, as long as it wasn't white powder.

I peeked into the first-class section and caught a glimpse of Monique's shapely leg. She had given me a nice, brief little wink as she passed by me during boarding. Thornton Rainey, right behind her, had squeezed himself into a brass-buttoned single-breasted dark suit that would have looked natty on a less repulsive fellow.

"Hey, Monique! Hey, Thornton! How's it goin', eh?" I had said in my hokiest Canadian accent.

"Hello, Cross," she said in her charming French voice. "Long time, no see, hey for?" Monique wore a sexy, clingy beige dress and no bra. Her magnificent breasts swayed freely, and I could feel the snake in my shorts start to uncoil.

I nodded yes. She went on her way; behind her, Thornton gave me a brusque little nod.

I sat back and closed my eyes for a few minutes. Soon I felt my jacket being opened and looked up to see Norm Freelan, the team's business manager, surreptitiously slipping an envelope into my pocket. I smirked a bit over my big pizza bill that had gotten him so ruffled.

"What's this?" I asked, snatching the envelope out of his hand.

"Lunch money," he said. "Breakfast, lunch and dinner, actually."

"My per diem?" I asked. Inside the envelope, I found fifty-five dollars in cash.

"That will have to last you the whole trip." Freelan, a timid, thirtysomething man with thinning blond hair, occupied the very bottom of the top. He seemed unable to keep anyone happy for long, including me.

"I don't fucking believe this! Fifty-five dollars for meals in

Manhattan? Freelan, you're screwing me! Help! Rape!"

"Keep your voice down."

"Kiss my ass, buddy. And tell Jacques and Warren to do the same."

"Tell them yourself. They're just on the other side of that curtain. I'm sure they would love to hear your grievances."

Our flight landed at LaGuardia and we left the aircraft. I shook Barrie half-awake and helped him out of the airliner and onto one of the buses waiting for us. Then he conked out again.

Most of us watched as Monique boarded one of the buses. We giggled and gasped as Thornton boarded, followed by Monique and then Snoop Kowalski. He cupped his hand on Monique's lovely bottom, ostensibly to assist her in boarding the vehicle. I had no idea why he did that, just as I had no clue as to what motivated Snoop in general. Monique wheeled around and slapped him so hard that we could hear the impact of her hand on his face. We threw back our heads and howled.

"Wow!" Wally Horton exclaimed. "I'd pay her half my salary to do that to me!"

Our bus inched its way into the cold, heart of New York City and restless shouts began from cranky hockey players.

"Focking driver!" Pavel, always the first to complain, started up. The people who could shut him up fast—Roderick, Warren and Jacques—sat in other buses. "I fly from Russia to New World faster than you get this piece of shit from airport to hotel! What's your problem, focker?"

Norm Freelan, sitting behind the driver, probably felt much of the sting of Pavel's venom. Nobody respected Freelan, because he dispensed petty cash for meals and did the endless flunky work of arranging for charter buses and hotel rooms. Since countless snafus were inevitable with the business of getting the buses and hotel rooms, players regularly swarmed about Freelan and deafened him with their shouted grievances.

"Freelan, motherfocker! If they don't have room for me to sleep, I come down and sleep with you. Are you bat boy or catcher?" Pavel once yelled at him.

By and by we made it into Midtown. Barrie gradually woke up and yawned as he oriented himself to his surroundings. "I'm gonna own this bitch!" he proclaimed in his best John Wayne voice.

"What bitch?" I asked.

"This bitch! New York! For the longest time, she's owned me. She's been my mum. But no more. I'm gonna make her my bitch."

"Do it, big man!" I said. "Make her your bitch!"

"You want her, too?"

"Maybe."

"You want her? You just say so. Uptown? Downtown? The Bowery? Harlem? We can do her together!"

"Yeah! Gimme that bitch! I'm gonna own her, too!"

"All right, then! We'll do this big bitch together!" he yelled, then made a sickly face and shook his head.

"I've got a bad hangover," he muttered.

He stayed mute for the rest of the bus ride to the hotel. We arrived at our hotel after dinnertime.

At the hotel, they gave me my room key, a plastic card. I sat in a lobby chair, took my iPad out of my knapsack and checked my emails. Monique wanted to meet me at a certain address in a few hours. I tapped the iPad a couple of times and got the local news service. New York had more going on, good and bad, in one week than Bayporte had in an entire year. After reading the sports section for a few minutes, I put the tablet back into my knapsack and took the elevator up to my room.

In the room, Barrie lay on one of the twin beds.

"The media here don't like us," I told him as I lay on my own bed. "They call us a bunch of 'syrup-sucking iceholes.'"

"At least they're not calling us 'steroid-shooting iceholes.'"

"Anything happening for you tonight?"

"Breeze said he would call." Breeze and Barrie had been friends in

Bayporte. Some time ago, Breeze, a high-class gangster of some kind, moved to Manhattan to evade the Mounties. Barrie said he missed Breeze and looked forward to hooking up with him in New York.

"Barrie," I asked, "what did you do to Harv do last night?"

"I took him out and showed him a good time."

"He looked very sick at the airport."

Barrie chuckled. "Poor boy. He just can't handle his good times."

I went to take a shower and get ready to see Monique. "Have you seen Snoop?"

"No. I hate that little maggot. He posted something online about how the three biggest assholes in Canadian history were serial killer Clifford Olson, Pierre Trudeau and me."

"I thought Trudeau was all right."

"Kiss my ass, Crossley. I'll never pass you the puck again."

I sighed and put my head under the hot spray. I kept thinking that if I called it quits with the Bullies, moved out to the Valley and spent the rest of my life with Laurel, I could stop sticking a needle into my ass and lying about it afterwards.

I went back into the bedroom. Barrie sat finishing up a call on his iPhone.

"That was Breeze," he said. "He's sending a car to come and get me. Wanna party with us?"

I shook my head. "I'm going to see Monique."

"Lucky you, screwing the fiancée of a rich guy."

"A fat, ugly, rich sack of shit who doesn't deserve such a grand girl."

"Breeze's car is supposed to be here by ten," Barrie said, reaching into his bag for his Bullies playbook. "I guess I should read this nonsense again, although to be honest with you, it really bores the living shit out of me."

"You don't need that playbook," I told him. "Just remember that if you have the puck and you're right in front of the other team's net, shoot it in."

Barrie made a cretinous face and said, "Duh."

"And tonight, if I have a hard-on and Monique has her legs spread—"

"*Score!*"

I took a taxi to see Monique. We drove past Central Park, and I thought for a moment about the Central Park jogger, the woman almost fatally victimized at nine or ten in the evening. What man or woman would go for a late-night run through that creepy place and honestly believe that the punks and sadists hiding in the bushes would leave them alone? Still, New York enchanted me, and I promised myself that one day I would bring Laurel here for daytime walks in Central Park and glamorous evenings of Broadway shows.

Sometime after ten I arrived at my destination, a chic apartment building on the Upper West Side. Monique sat waiting for me in the lobby. She wore a burgundy dress and proper heels. I had hoped she would wear something see-through.

"Where did you get that coat?" she asked, pointing to my leather overcoat, a garment that made me look like a 1970s pimp.

"What, this old thing? A department store gave it to me," I said.

"Got it for free, hey? Good deal," she said.

"Do you think I would have paid for something like this?" I asked, laughing. Monique laughed, too.

We got into the elevator and she said, "We're going to the penthouse. They're Adam's friends."

"And Adam is your friend?"

"Right."

The elevator slowed to a halt and we stepped out into a foyer at one end of which were double doors. "I'm going to miss these kinds of things," I said.

"What do you mean?"

"When you got engaged to Thornton, I decided to renounce every kind of wealth. I vowed to play hockey only as a public service. The NHL's first volunteer. Send my paycheck to the Salvation Army or the food bank."

"That's right. You're the guy they call a 'laff riot.'"

We knocked on the doors and an older woman answered it.

"Hello, I'm Tessa Goddard," she said. Tessa, stylish in a New Yorker kind of way, wore a floor-length sleeveless gown and had a salon tan. Her apartment occupied the top two floors of the building and a circular staircase connected the floors.

A svelte man with wispy gray hair came near us. He wore a turtleneck sweater under a tweed coat with suede elbow patches.

"He's the kind who subscribes to *Hustler* magazine under a phony name," I murmured to Monique.

"Don't be a smartass," she said. "He's my friend Adam."

"Monique!" Adam said as he lunged at her with an air kiss. "Lovely that you could make it."

I shook his hand, and his grip felt so tight that I thought he wanted to get me into a who's-tougher competition.

"My name is Adam Davidson," he said. "Chris Crossley? The hockey player? I've seen you on the ice."

"I spend a lot of time there."

He chuckled, then gave several examples of when he had seen me play. He had me confused with Barrie Weston. Monique's eyes floated about the room while I stood and listened to Adam as he gushed about Barrie's hockey prowess.

A squat, balding man came in and Adam went off to say hello.

"Who's the little guy?" I asked Monique.

"I don't know. Probably a writer."

"Maybe the *Harry Potter* author?"

"No, a woman wrote those books," she said.

"Then I guess that old guy isn't her. I would like to meet the *Harry Potter* lady someday, in case I ever need to borrow money."

We stood off to the side and watched the many people going up and down the staircase. They chattered as if they all knew each other.

One time at a party, I met a sportswriter from the Midwest who had gone through training camp with an NHL franchise. He spoke politely and intelligently about teams, players and statistics, but he had learned nothing about the one quality all NHL players share:

continuous terror. To me, the only people who really understand terror are soldiers and professional athletes. Warriors and jocks aren't normal people who go out to win a war or a game; we're warriors and jocks who go home after the battle and pretend we're normal people.

Most sportswriters don't know how it feels to lay in bed while hearing someone approach from down the hall, knowing that there might be a knock on the door and news that the player had just been traded or released. The sportswriter had never pondered how he would feel when his career ended, or how the end would come. Would he retire because he wanted to move on, or would his career end literally on the ice, as he lay there, muzzy or unconscious from a concussion?

Monique and I spotted the small, squat writer wandering around, checking us out. I didn't want to talk to him.

"That creepy man keeps looking at us," she said.

"He's in love with you. He wants to father your offspring. Let's go and find another party."

We did just that. It took us a few minutes to leave because so many people were between us and the doors.

In the elevator, Monique asked, "Cross, do you love me?"

"I love all people," I said.

"That's a stupid answer."

"I am a stupid man." I added, "Speaking of stupid men, are you really going to marry Thornton?"

"Why? Do you want to steal me away from him?"

"I would if I could. He can offer you far more than I can. I have given everything to the NHL. No, my dear, you just go ahead and marry your fat money man."

"OK. But you and I have had some fun times together, hey?"

I nodded.

"You'll still visit me once in a while?"

"You have my phone number."

The elevator stopped and its doors opened.

"Don't be so sad," Monique told me. "Marriage is just a part of life."

"Yeah, like death and taxes."

Just as we left the building we heard Barrie's booming voice and saw his formidable presence. "Thought we would join you!" he said as he and Breeze beamed at us. Monique asked the doorman to let us back in, and he did. We all got into the elevator: Monique and me, Barrie and Breeze, plus some little blonde they'd picked up. We all rode up to the party. Barrie and Breeze stood at the penthouse's open doorway, surveying the many people and waving at them like politicians running for office. Standing next to them, the chubby young blonde didn't seem to know where to look or wave. That didn't matter; everyone waved at Weston. Here, as everywhere else, Barrie made people forget about all others.

The short writer forced his way through to them and shook hands with Breeze, then Weston. The three men fell into a conversation that excluded everyone else. Barrie, Breeze and the blonde girl slowly went into the living room, Barrie a couple of steps ahead of the other two. The short writer promptly engaged Barrie in intense conversation.

The writer then took a few paces away from the others and assumed a hockey player's stance. He gripped an imaginary stick, dodging and darting as if evading invisible opponents. His movements had all the aplomb of a Jim Carrey comedy routine lampooning hockey. Barrie and Breeze looked at the man, then shook their heads at each other. Barrie walked away; he found me and Monique huddling in a corner.

"Chriscrosssss!" Barrie wore a regal-looking beige suit, another freebie from an upscale men's boutique grateful to have him appear in their ads. The chubby girl stood by him like a puppy.

"Who's this charming lassie?" I asked him. "First time I've seen her."

"She's my newest sweetie." He pulled her forward. "Sweetie, say hi to Chris Cross." He added, "Is there a can?"

"I think there's one over in the corner," I said.

"Let's go check it out, sweetie. I'm about to explode." He smiled at me and took the girl by elbow as the two went in search of a washroom.

Breeze stood talking to the lanky man, who scowled as Barrie and his new blonde sweetie walked by. Breeze finished talking to the man and rejoined us. Breeze, a handsome, muscular black man, knew some of the very top people in the NHL commissioner's office, if one could believe Barrie. Breeze had started a very exclusive adult-entertainment service in Manhattan and had grown adept at arranging good times for big spenders. Currently, he wanted to start procuring steroids and human growth hormone for New York teams.

"How's it going, Breeze?" I said, shaking his hand.

"Doing great, Cross," said Breeze. "I guess Barrie told you about some of my business dealings. I may be able to get you some products at a lower price than Simon's been charging you."

"This is Monique," I said, eager to change the subject.

Just then, Barrie and his sweetie returned from the washroom.

"New York is a crazy place, but I'm having a nice time," he said. "Breeze, you need to visit that bloody washroom. It's as big as an ice rink."

"Is anyone thirsty?" I asked.

"We have to split," Barrie said. "We have a car waiting outside and we're going to another party. Come with us, OK?" To his plump female companion he said, "Sweetie, you just stay here for the rest of the evening. There are lots of people here that's just dyin' to meet you. I have your number. I'll call you."

Soon we were back outside, crawling into a big black car. We took a few minutes to get comfortable, then the driver started up the car and pulled away from the curb. Although groping Thornton Rainey's fiancée around Manhattan seemed a spectacularly bad idea, I enjoyed myself a great deal. Our driver took us to some nightclub where dozens of people already stood in line, but the doorman just waved us on through. Inside, Denis Pilon did a striptease while dancing with a middle-aged woman, and Donny Bourdin sat with someone in a dark corner. Countless eyes shifted in our direction as Barrie Weston walked in.

Pilon waved at us while he continued getting naked.

"Bourdin is in the corner with some sweetie," I said to Barrie. "Maybe we better tuck them in before trouble starts."

Barrie rounded up both men and deposited them in the backseat of our car, and our driver locked them in. When Weston came back, Breeze ordered a round of drinks. Then Monique, pretending to be the restaurant robber in *Pulp Fiction*, hopped onto our table, waved an imaginary gun around the room and ordered all the customers to hand over their wallets or she would "execute every last motherfuckin' one of you." When the manager came by and ordered her to shut up and sit down, she obeyed him and sulked.

Barrie got a note from our server. A party of ten at another table wanted to meet him.

"Well, why not? If I was them, I would want to meet me, too." He got up and went to their table, all of them smiling and waving at him. Before any of them could stand up to greet him, he hopped onto their table and walked along it, reaching down to shake hands and saying, "Hi, I'm Barrie Weston, future Prime Minister of Canada." Accidentally or not, he kicked some of the half-full drink glasses into his admirers' laps.

"Nice to meet you," he said as he hopped off the table. "If you know where Canada is, be sure to come visit me."

Barrie sat down with us and said, "It always humbles me to go over and say hello to the common folk."

Breeze nodded and ordered more drinks.

Later, we went to another exclusive nightclub where the queue stretched down the block and the drinks cost ten dollars each. We ordered many rounds, ran up a substantial tab and ran off without paying. Next we went to a third exclusive nightspot, but instead of going inside, we stood on the sidewalk and passed joints back and forth.

We made it back to our hotel by sunrise, although we all had a bit of trouble getting out of the car. Pilon and Bourdin, after a brief nap, hustled up to their rooms. Monique hurried up to hers while I helped Barrie out of the car. Breeze had fallen into a deep slumber and stayed inside the vehicle. Out of the car and standing on the curb, Barrie took a puck out of his coat pocket and scribbled his name on it. He handed it to our driver, a black man.

"You're a credit to all colored people," Barrie said. "I wish there were more like you."

The man smiled and nodded, accepting the puck.

The car cruised away with the slumbering Breeze and we dashed into the lobby. The elevator's doors opened, and in it we discovered Jimmie Gish, our at-large coach, sitting in the corner, drunk and in tears.

"Assholes," he said, whimpering. "Fucking bastards."

"Jimmie," Weston said, reaching down and roughly shaking Gish's shoulder. "Wake up, guy. Get it together."

Gish looked up at him. "You laugh at me. You think I'm a joke."

"Nobody's laughing at you," Barrie said. "No one thinks you're a joke."

"Yes, you do." Gish snuffled some more. "You laugh at me behind my back, you assholes. Jacques hates me too."

The doors opened and we tried to help Gish out of there, but he slapped our hands away. Barrie and I left him on the floor, weeping and muttering to himself.

GEORGE ONSTOT

6

I woke up in my little hotel bed and noticed that Barrie wasn't in his, but I knew where to find him. I struggled to my feet and went into the bathroom to wish him good morning.

Barrie lay asleep in the bathtub, fully dressed, with a couple of bunched-up towels for pillows. I pulled the shower curtain to give myself some privacy as I sat on the throne.

"Mums don't let your sons grow up to play hockey," Barrie warbled. "Why do we stay out all night? Why do we stick needles in our asses?"

"So we'll play better and win some Stanley Cups," I said. "The bus leaves soon, you know."

We got dressed and went downstairs for breakfast.

I enjoyed walking through Madison Square Garden and thinking of all the famous people who had performed there: Sinatra, Elvis, the Beatles, Jimi Hendrix, the Doors, Michael Jackson and probably many world leaders. I wondered if they felt as honored to be there as I did. A performer couldn't hope for a much better venue than the Garden, even if the performer, like me, wasn't exactly the star of the show.

I opened my locker and began filling it. "The Garden," I murmured. "The Big Apple. Everyone's been here to make music, play sports, give speeches. I'll bet J.F.K. himself took a dump in the toilet I just used."

"What are you babbling about?" asked Jonny Curtiss, owner of the Bullies' most gigantic penis.

"Madison Square Garden is what I'm talking about, donkey-dick. It's a very important place, and I'm thrilled to be here, even though most of the people in the stands will keep forgetting that I'm here."

"Don't call me that name."

"Why not? When hockey is over for you, you'll have a great career in adult entertainment." Then, "Is your old lady still mad about the lipstick on your pecker?"

Donkey-dick threw one of his gloves at me.

I got undressed, put on a T-shirt and jockstrap and headed over to the training room.

"I need a rubdown," I said to Duncan McCallum. "I spent last night watching porno movies in Times Square and it left me pretty stiff."

"That's disgusting. But let me finish up with this guy and I'll do you."

I nodded and walked away. Our road workouts were mercifully brief. After a little while I went back to Duncan, who rubbed me with ointment until I feared I would burst into flames. He wrapped me instead of taping me and I climbed into my sweats.

The team lined up for calisthenics. Barrie Weston led us in jumping jacks and other exercises. The handsome, famous forward yelled out cadence in his robust Canadian accent. We finished with the jumping jacks and were going to split up into smaller units when Jimmie Gish spoke up.

"Do another set! We're all supposed to count the repetitions together. Why didn't you count, Crossley?"

Guilty as charged; I didn't count. Actually, due to my jet lag, I usually faked my way through many of these exercises. But I did do the jumping jacks and counted my repetitions, just like everyone else. Counting along helped team morale.

"I'm busted, Gish."

"If you want to be a comedian, Crossley," Jacques said, "go into show business. This is hockey. If you can't get with the program, don't even bother showing up."

"Sorry, Coach."

"Just for that," Gish called out, "everyone has to do another set. Pleased with yourself, Crossley?"

After we finished, I jogged past Gish and said, "I didn't count, Coach. I just pretended to."

"Asshole!"

I laughed and ran away.

Our practice was easy. When we were done, Jacques told us that those who wished to take the subway back to the hotel should feel free to do so. Why, I asked myself, would anyone want to take the subway when the bus sat parked outside, waiting for us? But only a few of us boarded the bus.

The rest of the day, we went to meetings and got timeouts for naps. Barrie and Breeze took Harv out for the evening and said they would be back before midnight.

Monique came up to our room before her date with Thornton. We went down on each other, but our loving lacked its usual thrill. After she departed, I told myself that maybe I should stop seeing her, considering her engagement to Thornton and my desire to be with Laurel.

A Bullies assistant stopped by to offer us sleeping pills. I started feeling anxious, as I always did when sleeping in a strange bed and having to play in a strange city where everyone would boo me. I took out my iPhone and touched Laurel's button, but she didn't answer. I crawled into bed and tapped on my iPad while some pretty boy TV anchor droned on about the day's tragedies. On my iPad, Apple announced its newest laptop computer, a shinier, sleeker MacBook than ever before. Well, they weren't going to sell me one of those things until my current MacBook crapped out, but that would certainly happen at some point. The iPad, however, I could do without once it bit the big one.

I peeked outside in the general direction of where the World Trade Center had stood. Plenty of lights out that way. I had read that back in the 1970s, many New Yorkers disliked the Twin Towers because they were too big and ugly, and others disliked the WTC because it wasn't really a world trade center—meaning an international bazaar—but instead functioned as an unaffordable office complex. After 9/11, the city's rulers spent several years arguing over what to build in its place; and there I stood at the window, just over a decade since the Twin Towers came down, and the new project, whatever it was, still hadn't been completed, and I hoped that the new project offered something for everyone, not just the world's moneyed elite. Of course, the moneyed elite were the people who really mattered, but I still hoped the common folk hadn't been forgotten.

Standing there at the window, I made up a joke:

Q: How many years does it take for New Yorkers to build a building?

A: Twelve. Ten to fight over what to build, and two to build the building.

At some point, Barrie stumbled in.

"Am I in trouble?" he asked.

"No bed check tonight."

"Good. I hate those bed checks, anyway. They make me feel like I'm a three-year-old who's misbehaving."

On TV, I found a 24-hour channel playing a martial arts marathon. Barrie and I got into our beds and fell asleep watching Steven Seagal kick the shit out of the bad guys ten at a time.

GEORGE ONSTOT

7

Barrie picked up the phone just as it started to ring for our wake-up call. He muttered into the phone and hung up.

"Morning already?" I asked, my head still full of sleep.

"Getting late," he said. "We have breakfast in a little while, devotional after that, then the game shows. Works out really nice, hey?"

Barrie loved the TV game shows, especially *Jeopardy!* He downloaded them a dozen at a time and always played along. He believed that those shows had nearly doubled his I.Q. He sprang out of bed and headed for the washroom. I stayed in bed and pondered the meaning of my dream.

My dream was this: I was late for the game, the buses had gone and I couldn't get a cab because they were all full. I couldn't find Madison

Square Garden, but I could hear everyone chanting "Chriscross! Chriscross!" After a while I got a ride with John Lennon, who conceded that the Garden could be a good hangout, but he had more fun being the ghost of the Dakota. He slowed down in front of the Garden so I could get out, he wished me luck and sped off. I groped my way to the darkened dressing room; I could scarcely see, but heard rats and mice scratching and clawing about. I wanted to say to hell with it and go back to the hotel.

Then I noticed I was standing naked in the penalty box. Everyone stared at me. Tommy, our clubhouse guy, held my gear over his head as he stood in the other team's penalty box. He smiled and waved; I crept across the ice barefoot, and Barrie flipped the puck to me, but since I had no stick, I could only catch it with my bare hands. I wondered what he, and everyone else, expected me to do. I kept walking on the ice, scarcely feeling its coldness, until finally Jacques told me to pass the puck to one of my teammates and return immediately to our penalty box. I did, and as soon as I sat on the bench a huge image of my penis and testicles appeared on the stadium's screen. The crowd screamed with laughter.

"Get up, guy," Barrie said as he got dressed.

I immediately got out of bed. "We can wear whatever we want this morning, right?"

"Yes, but no skirts, dresses or high heels."

Downstairs, the big board said that Manhattan Rooms I and II had been reserved for us.

"Yummy," I said as we went inside. "Breakfast is my favorite meal. Especially after a night of good lovin'." Nearly all of our teammates sat waiting to eat. Barrie walked past me and entered the room as he loudly hummed a country song, his way of saying, "I have arrived." I stood aside and waited for Barrie to make some crucial decisions, such as where we would sit. As team captain, he knew the significance of selecting the appropriate table at which to tell his corny jokes and boost the morale of the anxious men surrounding him. He seldom explained to me why he chose to eat with certain players or at certain tables. I didn't eat with him whenever he sat with players who hated me.

The hotel attendants had pulled back a sliding partition, making one vast room of Manhattan 1 and 2. We used one section for breakfast; in another, Duncan and his assistants looked after us. In a corner of the huge room, a white board and podium faced a few rows of chairs. Jacques always liked to hold last-moment meetings, and naturally we had a team devotional.

Barrie sat down to breakfast with Vlad, Pavel, and some others. I sat with Donny Bourdin and Mark Ignas.

"Hey, Cross." Donny offered me a high five. I gave his hand a sloppy, sweaty little slap. "How are you doing? Not letting the bastards grind you down, hey?"

"Never," I lied.

"Just have to stay positive," he said. "You sure you're feeling alright?"

"If I get to feeling any better, they'll give me a drug test."

Donny laughed. A server came by and placed on our table a platter heaped with steaks and scrambled eggs, probably the worst shit imaginable before engaging in strenuous physical activity. The food doesn't get digested, it just sits in your stomach and rots because the brain, out of pregame terror, instructs the internal organs to redirect the blood to other parts of the anatomy

"Check it out," Donny said, gesturing to a platter of food. They probably had put yellow food coloring into the eggs to make them look more appetizing. Maybe they had done the same thing to the steaks, too. Sometimes they put in too much coloring and the food didn't look real.

"Breakfast of champions," I muttered, staring at the food as the server delivered platters of steaks and eggs to each table. Some of the Bullies laid into her, much the way they tormented the bus driver who took us to the hotel.

"Hey sweetie," Vlad called to her, loudly enough for everyone in Manhattan 1 and 2 to hear, "is this the best you got for us? You got sweeter meat for us someplace else, hey?"

She pretended to ignore him but silently cussed him out as she continued putting platters on all tables and wiping sweat from her forehead.

"She works hard for the money," Vlad sang loudly and tunelessly, making some of the Bullies laugh.

Soon we all had plenty of steaks and eggs on our plates. Hungry or not, we ate generous portions. The food would sit in your stomachs until well after game time and be digested as we slept, or we would vomit before then, perhaps even on the ice.

At just before ten, I covertly popped a couple of pills.

"Juice?" Bourdin asked, his voice quiet.

"Affirmative."

"Still using a needle, too?"

"Naturally."

"Good man. You the guy who put up that message that got Jacques pissed off?"

"Not me." I shot a look at Ignas, who winked at me.

"Juicing isn't the worst thing," Donny said. "Fucking around with uppers and downers? That's suicidal. Do you remember Tony Hall?"

"Sure." Tony Hall, a journeyman defenseman, had spent half a season with us after wandering about the NHL for close to a decade. By the time he joined us, his skills had mostly eroded, but he did his best for us.

"I heard that Tony's idea of preparation for a game was to take painkillers and uppers together," Donny told me. "The combination made him feel indestructible. He said he could get knocked on the ice and get a major concussion but wouldn't feel it."

"I have to admit that my own pills and needles have made me better than I ever thought I could be," I said. "I'm not sure how long I can keep it up."

"Tony probably has neurological problems now." Donny checked his watch. "I think we have a meeting in a few minutes. Harri Krishna will be speaking to us this morning."

I sneered. "Harri Krishna."

Harri "Krishna" Singh, famous for being famous, had come into our lives a few years earlier. He had taken a particular, and peculiar, interest in saving our souls—especially mine, which I believed required no saving. Dressed in collarless shirts buttoned all the way up and dark blazers, he went around blessing everyone in our training camp and being everybody's newest best friend; he insisted that everyone call him by his first name. He had a medical, not a divinity degree, and Jacques had asked him to come speak to us about.

Harri admonished us about the foolishness of failing to go through life without a relationship with Him. Harri told us about his years as an obscure New Delhi physician whose patients showed him little gratitude for curing their diseases and saving their lives. He said that, in order to have the gratifying and fulfilling career he truly wanted, he needed to have friends in higher places. So he cultivated a relationship with the Friend in the Highest of All Places, and he got the life he desired and felt he deserved as a staff physician at a private American hospital. In return for being a warm, concerned caregiver, Harri received a generous salary and very astute advice on how to invest his income.

Upon becoming independently wealthy, he wanted to see fewer nasty patients, make even more money and become famous. He wrote a book, *My God, My Self,* a hundred or so pages of his own spiritual advice, fleshed out with a hundred or more blank pages for his readers to chart their own progress on their quests for nirvana. In his own search for new souls to conquer, Harri came upon us, the Bayporte Bullies on TV, punching the bejesus out of their opponents.

'These men are needing my help,' he said.

Jacques and Harri became quite friendly. Jacques wanted some favors from the Man Upstairs. Harri wanted to get to know these violent hockey players, and insisted on speaking to us just before games.

He asked me why I had eschewed the devotionals. I told him that God had more important work to do than worry about getting us our first Stanley Cup. In response, Harri started making his talks a bit more colorful, going on about pretty girls and bar hopping.

I always swore profusely around Harri. I winked at him, blew kisses and, when I could, farted loudly. I told him there was no God and that he seemed quite a fool to think otherwise. But Harri always came prepared, and he came to my defense whenever one of the Bullies' zealous Christians, angered by my misbehavior, threatened to send me up to meet Jesus right there and then.

Jacques, pushing aside his plate of steak and eggs, stood up and told us all that the meeting and devotional would be delayed for half an hour or so. He didn't say why. I glanced over at Barrie, who muttered something about being late in getting to his game shows because of the delay.

When the meeting ended and Harri got up to speak, Barrie and I got up and walked out. We walked right past Harri and I gave him a little bye-bye wave.

"Harri Krishna looked mad," Barrie said. He had given Harri that nickname because Harri's bald head, dark skin and glasses reminded him of a Hare Krishna. Harri reminded me of Gandhi, if Gandhi had been chubby and alcoholic.

"He'll probably let Harv Arthur stand at the podium to do some talking about sin, salvation and short-handed goals," I said.

As we stood at the elevator, Barrie hung his head and asked himself or me, "Why is it so hard being me?"

As he watched his game shows, I packed my belongings, stuffed my MacBook into my knapsack and took a taxi to the Garden. Barrie remained in our room and read the day's news on his iPad. He would travel on the team bus later on that morning.

Players like Barrie and me, who had sustained no major injuries over the years, could go show up later for games because they required no special attention from Duncan. I showed up early because I liked being in the Garden. One of our recent acquisitions, Rocky Ramos, a third-liner from the Dallas Stars, came in early just to "get ready to get busy." Ramos would take uppers and sit in the locker room, his body trembling from the drugs and his mouth jabbering whatever thoughts his overheated brain generated. I often sat next to him and listened to his accounts of sexual encounters, gang fights and hockey games. He guzzled water, yawned and stretched; now and then he would grab his shoulders and rock back and forth like autistic children I had seen on television. In the occasionally frigid Bayporte winters Duncan would make Rocky stand outside to cool down the guy's body.

Poor Rocky, I thought.

The taxi to Madison Square Garden took me through midtown Manhattan.

"Don't you think you're getting there early?" asked the driver.

"Better early than late," I replied.

"I saw the Rangers last week, when they played the Bruins. You know what? The Rangers suck. I don't think I'll live to see them win another Stanley Cup."

"At least they've won a couple already."

"That visiting team? They've got a goddamn good nickname for a hockey team. The Bayporte Bullies!" He honked his horn and cackled. "The goddamn Bayporte Bullies. Hahaha!" He asked, "Where *is* Bayporte, anyway?"

"Somewhere in Canada, I think."

He nodded. "Yeah, you're probably right."

When we reached the Garden, I saw a few Bayporte personnel unloading bulky items.

"Cross, help us with these," Duncan said.

"Yeah." I got all my personal things in one hand and got two of theirs in the other one. I headed over to the high-security entrance and, in a girlish voice, said to the guard, "I'm with the band."

"Excuse me?"

"I'm with the team." I gave him my steeliest Dirty Harry squint.

"Go ahead," he said.

Look at 'em like you mean business, my older brother had always told me. Good advice from a fool. After years as a mining-company CEO and family man, he had reconnected with his high school sweetie on Facebook and run off with her. She came back, saying

he'd gone to South America.

Rather than do the usual thing and head for the locker room, I went to check out the ice I would be skating on. Sitting in one of the premium seats, I watched the ice crew, all of them bent over, as meticulous as surgeons, smoothing out a portion of the playing surface. In another part of the facility, a TV team set up its hardware. One of the guys spoke into his radio to the boys in the van outside, talking about what hockey freaks across the continent would see today. Close to the Rangers' bench, a few men stood around pointing to the ice and gestured around the Garden. One of them, Canadian hockey icon Wayne Gretzky, had played for the New York Rangers.

Now, as ever, I gazed at the ice and wondered how I would feel at game time, playing in a foreign country, taking on the bad guys, being booed by the whole house. A couple of kitchen employees in soiled aprons and sweated-through shirts bounded down towards me and looked around.

One of them, a tall, chubby man, brightened up. "Wow! Do you see that?" he asked the other guy. "That's Wayne Gretzky on the other side of the ice!"

"Which guy?" asked the other man, short and skinny.

"The guy in the fur coat."

"Oh, now I see him. Hey! Wayne! Wayne Gretzky! Number ninety-nine!" He waved and smiled.

Gretzky looked up, hearing his name called.

"Ninety-nine! Suit up and get ready! We're gonna need you against those Bullies!" yelled the tall, fat kitchen worker.

The Hall of Famer, who had spent four seasons in a Rangers

uniform, waved and smiled, then promptly went back to his discussion.

"Hell of a guy," said the fat man as they started to go back to work. "Hell of a guy."

The skinny guy nodded but somehow seemed disturbed as they walked by me.

"Do you know what I heard? I heard that Gretzky had a rhinoplasty."

"A what?" asked the fat guy.

"A rhinoplasty. A nose job. Do you think it's true?"

The fat guy shrugged. "Well, him and his old lady live in Hollywood. All those people get facelifts and nose jobs, boob jobs, butt jobs. You notice he still has all his hair? Maybe he wears a rug, too. You never know about those famous people."

"Still, he ain't very handsome."

"He's Gretzky. He don't gotta be handsome."

The two men walked away.

I scanned the rink, trying to determine its overall condition, but of course I could tell nothing until I actually skated on it. I thought of using my newer skates but that decision could wait till later. The football and baseball players had it worse. Some fields, used for football and baseball, probably weren't especially good for either sport.

Football players had to know that mud cleats were good for soggy fields but potentially hazardous for dry ones. In hockey, at least for me, ice skates needed only to have sharp blades and a snug fit. Football players said that those artificial surfaces were as hard as concrete. How those tackles must hurt! Fortunately, my choice of skates made little difference. I needed only to score goals and please Jacques LaPierre.

I've heard people say that a player should retire when he can't remember the last time he felt well. Jet lag aside, I had no major or chronic problems, no broken bones or torn ligaments. In college, some of my teammates sustained severe injuries that disqualified them from NHL careers.

"Where the fuck did you go?" demanded Duncan. "You have all

my stuff!"

"Sorry about that," I said. "It's a big place and I lost my way." I returned his equipment bag and sat down by my locker. My brain started getting into fight mode. I could practically feel the adrenalin squirting into my bloodstream to make the right chemical balance for me to get through the game with as little damage as possible. I felt very tired and wanted to go back to my hotel room for a long nap; instead, I started to take off my clothes and slowly got ready to suit up.

The concrete felt ice-cold under my bare feet, so I sat on a bench and put my feet up.

I looked around to see who else had come in. Wally Horton sat as Duncan taped him up. Horton, by his own admission an insufferable, lifelong tormentor of others—and therefore a natural hockey player—considered me his best friend on the team for turning him on to Winstrol and Dianabol. He needed the tape because of injuries he had sustained due to his highly aggressive style of playing hockey. I didn't know if he could play without being taped up. Tape, a hockey player's best friend. Many guys had been surviving for years on tape and drugs.

Rocky Ramos sat in the recliner, and, judging by his face and restless limbs, I guessed he had already taken his pregame pills. We gave each other the subtlest wave but said nothing.

I looked into my locker and began checking out my equipment. Our equipment manager had already sorted out my stuff—my shoulder pads sat on the top shelf, and my gleaming helmet squatted in the neck hole. My short pants and sweater hung from hooks.

On my locker's floor I found my skates, neatly shined and freshly sharpened, and an abundant supply of knee, thigh, forearm, elbow and hip pads made of rubber and plastic. The team had them made up for everyone who wanted them, and I used them religiously at first, but started trying to play without them because they were bulky and slowed me down. Sometimes I fantasized about playing naked, with just my skates and stick.

"Cross!" Duncan McCallum called out. "Want a rubdown?"

"Let's do it."

He began spreading analgesic on the backs of my legs, then did my back. I stood up and he wrapped both thighs with bandages to retain heat. Afterwards, I went back to my locker, smoked a cigar and scrolled through my iTunes library for my pregame playlist. I couldn't remember the lyrics to half of these songs, but their melodies and tempos energized me. Half of them seemed to be sung by Michael Jackson or Elvis Presley.

Ahahahahaboomboom......

I put on my silver short pants, then my socks and black sweater and appraised myself in the mirror. Whoever selected our team colors had been smart to decide on silver and black; even when we played badly, we looked tough. I lay on the bench with a pad for a pillow and closed my eyes, listening to the people around me—trainers, players, insignificant stadium attendants, all of them yakking about things as diverse as how many more times Tom Cruise would marry to when the next NHL strike or lockout would happen. My music pounded out of the weak laptop speakers:

Nanananayeahyeahyeahyeah.....

I breathed deeply and tried to settle down. The chemicals swirling around in my brain conjured up images of body checks, power plays, grunting defensemen and Laurel English.

I stubbed out my cigar and my music continued. Sitting up, I laced up my skates and stared at them for the longest time. With ice skates, more than other items, you get what you pay for, and I always got the very best ones.

Boomboomuhuhuhuh....

A door burst open and some teammates bounded in, dressed in suits and carrying briefcases, as if they were real estate hustlers following the scent of money. The group of hockey players so corporately dressed made me think of a conventional of insurance agents.

My teammates' racket made me nervous. Game time approached, and I mentally reviewed Jacques' adjustments for the offense that had us banging in so many goals.

Yahahahaunhunhunh.....

I turned off my MacBook as a coach arrived with extra instructions, but the music still did its bump-and-grind in my mind. I also thought about sexy women in the stands and a big night in Manhattan after the game.

"All first-liners on the ice in ten minutes!" the man said.

"Do you want some B-12, Cross?" asked Duncan McCallum.

"Negative," I replied. "They make me cry and run home to Mum."

I watched while he stuck a vitamin needle into Wally Horton, who still had a puffy face from punching it out with Vlad a few days earlier. Then Pavel Pavlovich bent over, ready for his shot. The doctor plunged the needle into the big man's buttock, and Pavel looked ready to cry.

I stood around and observed my teammates blink, grind their teeth and lick their lips, the way they always did when feeling the effects of Winstrol. Vlad Rybka, not a juicer, yawned and scratched himself from whatever drugs he had just taken, and Wally Horton kept blinking. They looked like a couple of mental patients to me. Most of the time, they acted that way, too.

Roderick Rainey came bounding in, beaming and waving, flanked by Harri. The two men worked the room, giving pats, smiles and good wishes to us Bullies. I turned my back to them and they walked past me, although as they left I saw Harri pull a bottle of pop out of the ice chest and drink it down in thirty seconds. Hangovers could really dehydrate people.

Barrie sat against the wall, contemplating the fans, the game plan, the Bullies and Jacques. I needed to piss, but the urinals were occupied. Pregame anxiety often caused us diarrhea and vomiting; the stench repelled everyone except those who needed to use the toilets. I forced myself to breathe through my mouth and tears streamed down my face as I urinated.

A stall door swung open and I heard Mark Ignas' voice.

"Crossley, I need your help."

He had a syringe.

"Help me, OK?" he asked, his voice hushed.

I smirked.

He snarled. "I don't want anyone to see me juicing up."

"I don't want anyone to watch me, either, but everyone knows I do it."

"Just help me."

I nodded and stuck the needle into his rear. "Are you careful about your dosages? You don't want bitch tits."

"First line on the ice right now!" someone shouted.

We hurried up his injection and headed out into the arena to a chorus of boos as soon as the crowd saw our unmistakable black jerseys and silver short pants.

"I'm really glad we're going into the postseason this year," I said to Barrie above the noise of the crowd.

"It won't mean shit if we don't go all the way and win the Cup," he said.

"Did you enjoy *Wheel of Fortune* this morning?" I asked.

"It was OK. On the bus ride over, Jacques really ragged on me about getting up and walking out just as Harri Krishna was about to say his stuff."

"Didn't you explain to him that your game shows came first?"

"Barrie! Barrie!" the people cried out. The New York fans loved him as much as they could love the enemy. NHL fans in general loved him. If he didn't play for the Bullies, the Rangers would certainly try to snap him up.

We stood in our penalty box for a moment. Harri presently joined us.

"How come you boys took off on me before the devotional?" he asked, smiling.

"We were beating off to porno videos," I said.

Harri chuckled. "As long as you had a good reason for your absence."

Barrie and I got out on the ice and skated on the clean, shiny ice. I could hear vendors walking up and down the aisles, selling beer, hot dogs and peanuts. Dreadful canned music came out of the public address system. The crowd grew noisier as the first few Rangers emerged. Bob Kursar, their captain, skated to center ice. Barrie and I went over to him.

"Hey, Barrie, hey, Cross," he said. "How's it goin'?"

"We're surviving, Bob," Barrie said. "How's your new boss?"

The Rangers had fired their head coach at the beginning of the season and replaced him with one of their executives, a former player and charismatic personality who, as head coach, had been winning in spite of himself. We would probably play against them in the Stanley Cup finals, if we got that far.

"Nice enough guy, I guess," Bob said. "No dumber than the other NHL coaches and smarter than one or two. We're owned by a consortium, you know, and they have no use for losers, so they called a meeting and demanded a new head coach. They settled the matter internally by making one of our suits try to manage the team." He shook his head. "I guess it didn't occur to them to hire away an experienced head coach from another team. At least with the Bullies, I don't imagine you have these kinds of problems. Rainey probably doesn't breathe down Jacques' neck all the time as long as you win games."

"You wouldn't like Jacques," Barrie said. "He eats his young."

"I heard that about Roderick Rainey. See ya." Bob took off to join his teammates.

"They know our owner is a homosexual pedophile," I said.

"Good news travels fast," Barrie retorted.

The rest of the Bullies came out and we began skating in circles, shooting pucks at Mike Fillo. He calmly stopped most of them, although Barrie lined up a wrist shot that sailed into the net and left Fillo spread-eagled and humiliated.

"Wow!" I shouted, thrilled by Weston's slick shot. Even when jetlagged, Barrie could surprise me.

Jacques got us all off the ice and back into the dressing room for a few final items of business. Everyone milled around or grumbled.

"All right, gentlemen," Jacques said. "Be sure to put your hand over your heart during the two national anthems. You might even feel compelled to show good manners and sing along with the fans." He admonished us about not using profanity or scratching our testes, especially on camera. I didn't sing along during the American national anthem because I didn't like the song, and I often didn't sing along to O Canada because I couldn't remember the words.

Then Harri stepped up to speak and we all bowed our heads.

"Dear Lord, please bless these men as they prepare to meet their competition…" Harri, it seemed, wanted the Almighty to intercede on our behalf as we mixed it up with the Rangers. If so, wasn't some holy man in the other dressing room, at that moment, asking Him to fix things for *them?*

He went on to thank God for getting us safely to New York and for the privilege of playing this day in the United States. Harri told Him that none of us cared much about winning, as if one could lie to the Creator. I nearly burst out laughing at that one, just as I experienced a little inner giggle when he said something about our sound minds and bodies; we were all amped up on juice or something else. Then Harri blessed the entire Rainey family and asked us to join in the Lord's Prayer.

I peeked out the tiniest bit, to ensure that nobody caught me not praying mode. I saw a bit of smoke lingering off to the side, and then noticed Barrie sitting off to the side, taking a cigarette break, bored shitless or supremely confident; with him, you could never be sure.

"…Amen," said Harri.

"Let's go fuck 'em up!" Wally Horton cried out. He added, "Sorry about that. I got a bit carried away."

"Your enthusiasm is understandable," replied Harri.

"Remember what I said about good manners during the national anthems," Jacques said as his players headed out towards the rink. An *American Idol* pop tart struggled through both anthems. I thought for a minute or two about Laurel English and her late husband, who had died for nothing in Afghanistan.

While the teams stood at attention for the national anthems, Barrie and I sat off to the side, I fiddled with a puck, my hands so clumsy that I dropped it a few times. I couldn't remember much of what we'd covered about the Rangers' defense, and I started to regret not wearing my other skates, especially as the ice got rougher and more scratched up.

I kept toying with the puck, dropped it once more, and decided that I had put on the wrong pair of skates. I crept past my teammates and trainers, and it occurred to me that I was the only person in Madison Square Garden not standing at attention. Then I changed my mind about my skates and stood there, awkward as hell, waiting for the American national anthem to end.

A sense of embarrassment swept through the crowd as the fans finished the song before the pop tart did. The crowd half-booed her as she wrapped up her performance with a strained little smile.

The fans made plenty of noise as the first-liners from both teams converged on the ice.

The face-off started; the crowd roared when the Rangers initially got the puck, then the fans quieted down as Vlad Rybka checked a Ranger against the boards and stole away the puck. But the Rangers got it back for a couple of minutes, although they couldn't get it out of their own zone, and they all tried to avoid Vlad. When three Rangers and one Bully crowded around the boards and the puck became lodged between them, a referee blew his whistle and called for a faceoff.

Denis Pilon and Bob Kursar bent over, their sticks twitching like agitated limbs, as the referee dropped the puck. Pilon for a moment seemed to have it, but then inadvertently knocked the little black disk into the air, where it sat suspended as if frozen for hours before dropping in front of a Rangers forward. The Ranger glanced around for a moment, then broke away and slapped the puck just past our diving Mike Fillo. Jacques screamed at Pilon as all the Rangers raised their sticks in celebration.

Following the network-ordered timeout to sell Hummers, beer and hard-on pills, Jacques calmed down a bit. Our next faceoff pitted me against Rudy Sperling. I won the puck, passed it to Barrie and he passed it to Vlad, who bobbled it. Sperling came into steal it, but Vlad slashed him with his stick; the referee sent Vlad to the penalty box for two minutes. Jacques screamed some more as his big Russian defenseman skated over and sat down.

New York immediately began a power play with their one-man advantage. Within seconds they had three men passing the puck to each other as around our goalie, trying to stuff the puck past him. Then the five Rangers surrounded Fillo, their frenzied activity like a movie gangbang. With twenty seconds to go in their power play, the red scoring light went on. The Rangers jumped all over each other as if they had just won the Cup. New York 2—Bayporte 0.

Barrie skated over to our bench and glowered at the scoreboard. He, Jacques and I had one of the mini-huddles we were so fond of. "Play it off the boards," Jacques said. We both nodded and headed for the faceoff. Barrie won control of the puck, passed it to me and I headed for the boards, and my teammates waited for the pass along the boards. Jacques had the right idea. I passed it to Pilon, who passed it back to me once I got behind the net. With all the chaos on the ice, the Rangers' goalie, Gordy Roeske, apparently didn't know the puck's location and looked around as I half-kicked the puck towards him and shoved it into the net. It wasn't pretty, but it worked. New York 2—Bayporte 1.

During that shift Weston dazzled us all with his agility and grace, and we all smiled as we got off the ice to make way for the second-liners. Harv Arthur and the others got on the ice and did the usual give-and-take with the Rangers, but Harv managed to tie the game with a breakaway goal. The third line came on and finished the first period. New York 2—Bayporte 2.

We went to the locker room. Being tied, of course, beat the shit out of being behind.

Cans of Coke and Pepsi sat on ice for our enjoyment. Most of the players drank Pepsi, though I liked Coke. Juicing had increased my stamina, even after a really vigorous shift on the ice. I couldn't wait to get my ass out there and take it to the Rangers.

Some players sat on benches, or on the floor, smoking and drinking pop. Barrie sat next to me, smoking a Player's and guzzling a Pepsi. He hummed a pretty song and blew out a long stream of smoke. His confidence inspired me, but his cigarette smoke did not. I had to move over to the shower room.

The intermission lasted long enough for our bodies to stiffen from sitting around with nothing to do, while hockey freaks at home watched retired sports superstars hawk products with practiced sincerity. Too many teams got slow and lazy during intermissions, their minds wandering off to sex, drugs and rock-'n'-roll.

I frowned as Pavel took a small handful of uppers. The pills wouldn't kick in until the third period or later, and would probably get their mightiest grip on his mind after the game, when they would induce in him the world's most severe case of verbal diarrhea, especially if he had combined the uppers with liquor. Pavel, in a voice loud enough to be heard from half a mile away, would spout his shocking philosophy of life, a cross between Caligula and Adolf Hitler.

Most of the team got up and started wandering around. A referee came in and said we had five minutes left.

"All right," Jacques said to us all. "This game has been more challenging than we might have wanted, but remember that we will probably play this team for the Stanley Cup fairly soon. We need to be more aggressive and bear down on them."

The fans had returned to their seats, balancing hot dogs, submarine sandwiches and liquid refreshments on their laps. For the thousandth time, I felt grateful that we played indoors, where weather always ceased to be a factor.

The second period started out poorly. We won the faceoff but Bob Kursar stole the puck and slapped it in from twenty feet away past a napping Mike Fillo. Rangers 3—Bullies 2.

After that, I looked up at the clock often, hoping we could stuff one in and tie it again before the second line replaced us; for some reason, we played much better when we weren't behind. Neither team seemed to be able to do much with the puck following Kursar's slap shot; we got it, lost it, regained it and lost it again. I felt bitterly frustrated, and began to loathe the NHL, Roderick Rainey, Jacques, Barrie Weston and the rest of the team.

At the beginning of the third period, Jacques said, "Crossley, you stay in for the rest of the game."

"Yes, Coach," I replied, looking to Barrie Weston for ways of winning this game.

"You in for the duration?" he asked me.

"Absolutely."

He nodded. "Good. Maybe you should provoke the Rangers into slashing you and then they'll get a penalty. We'll get a man advantage."

Barrie's bright idea took away some of my fun. I hated provoking the opposition, mostly because *I* usually ended up in the penalty box. I also hated engaging in fisticuffs despite playing a sport in which physical altercations were common.

I watched Donny Bourdin retrieve the puck from our end and skate towards center ice, going so fast and single-mindedly that he didn't see the big Ranger slam into him head-on, nearly knocking off Bourdin's helmet. Bourdin fell on his ass, the Ranger stood over him, perhaps wondering if the Bully was dead, and I felt overjoyed at the sight of the loose puck floating about at center ice as the Rangers' goalie skated out of his crease and pointed at Bourdin. Then I felt guilty at my own pleasure over Bourdin's misfortune as I rushed over to the puck and fired it into the empty net. The red scoring light went on, the horn sounded and I pumped my arm in victory. Jacques and our trainer rushed out of the penalty box to attend to Bourdin, who remained flat on his back. I was ashamed of myself for being so grateful to get that scoring opportunity as I watched Jacques and Duncan help Bourdin off the ice. Still, it counted: Rangers 3—Bullies 3.

The third period continued, and we were trailing. The Rangers had the puck, and Kursar began dancing around the tired Bullies for a couple of minutes, ending up behind our net. But then Pavel and Horton trapped him and the referee blew the puck dead.

I skated over to Jacques and told him I needed to take a piss break.

"They've called a commercial break," he said. "Be quick about it."

I nodded and headed for the washroom. As I passed through the locker room, I saw Duncan and some others standing over Bourdin, who lay stretched out on a table on his stomach, mumbling or whimpering. The doctor kept kneading the backs of Bourdin's legs, as if his hamstrings were the problem.

Bourdin looked away from us. He still had his helmet on, though it had been bent out of shape. I went up to him and heard his attempts at speaking. I put my hand on his shoulder and tried to explain that he shouldn't worry or cry; we were going into the postseason and would win a Stanley Cup. I surprised myself by how much of a cheerleader I could be when I considered it necessary.

Bourdin turned his head and faced me. His face, covered with blood, now looked hideously disfigured. His skin had a purplish hue, shiny and lumpy, as if he'd been made up for a Hollywood horror movie.

"Dammit!" I barked. "It's his face, not his legs. Someone get over here and fix him up!"

The doctor and trainers, startled, came over right away to examine Bourdin's face.

"Hope he didn't bite his tongue," the doctor said, removing Bourdin's headgear and forcing open his mouth. "May need surgery. Better get him to a hospital right away."

"What's the problem?" Jacques asked, standing in the doorway.

"His face got rearranged," said the doctor. "We're going to put him in the ambulance."

"I guess he's through for the season," Jacques said, walking away.

I heard the noises indicating that the washroom-and-beer breaks were over and the hockey game would resume imminently. Stepping back from Bourdin, I tried to listen to the sounds of the game but couldn't stop looking at my critically wounded teammate whose blackish blood now stained the concrete floor.

The puck sailed over the glass and into the stands and I skated over to Weston at center ice.

"Shit." I flashed back on how Bourdin's handsome face had been reduced to something resembling pulverized fruit. "Did you see what happened to Bourdin?"

"I don't want to hear about it," Barrie retorted.

We all looked tired and cranky. Weston and Kursar took their time about getting ready for the faceoff. Everyone just wanted to finish and go home.

"Hey, Denis," said Wally Horton, "don't puke up the puck this time if you get it."

"Kiss my ass, Horton. You just do your job and I'll do mine."

"Shut up, both of you," Barrie said. "I'm the boss, so I'll do the talking. If you don't like it, tough titties."

I glanced around at my teammates. Some of them had probably already started wondering about how they would explain themselves to Jacques when he showed them their goofs on the big screen during the next meeting. Angry and embarrassed, they probably just wanted to rest up for the postseason, which would begin in several days.

The puck dropped. Barrie got it, passed it to Vlad, who watched as it traveled right between his legs and onto a Ranger's stick.

"Dammit, Vlad, wake up!" screamed Horton as they raced after the Ranger who had the puck.

"Fock you, too, Horton! Who make you the boss, hey?"

"You guys hear me?" Barrie shouted. "I'm the boss. When I'm on the ice, shut up!"

We stole the puck and managed to move it around the Rangers' net, and Pilon passed it to Barrie, who shot it right into the glove of Roeske, the Rangers' goalie. Then the whistle blew.

"What the fuck!" Pilon yelled.

"Sorry about that, Denis," Barrie said.

"Sorry doesn't mean shit," Denis said.

"Everybody, shut up!" Barrie hollered. "I'm going to say it again: I'm the boss, so be quiet unless I ask you something."

"Why can't you idiots get your shit together?" Horton asked.

"What did you just say? Did I hear you right?" Weston asked, incredulous. "One more word out of you and you're history."

"Like hell," Horton said.

Weston glowered at Horton for a moment or so, then skated over to the referee and asked for a timeout. Weston headed towards our bench and spoke to Jacques. None of us said anything, and we certainly didn't look at the fuming Wally Horton, as we awaited Barrie's return. Finally I looked at Mark Ignas, who smiled and nodded. I smiled and nodded back. Jacques turned to Jonny Curtiss and gestured for him to go in. The crowd booed as Curtiss came in and Horton left, and Horton looked so enraged that I thought he might swing his stick at Weston or Jacques.

"I thought he'd never leave," Barrie said. "Give us your best, Curtiss. I want to beat these clowns in front of their own fans. We need to keep the puck in their zone for the rest of the game. Think you can help us with that?"

"I'll do what I can," said Curtiss, his limbs trembling.

"Just get ready to score," Barrie said.

On the faceoff, Kursar got the puck but lost it soon enough to Ignas, who passed it over to me in the Rangers' zone. They had as many players on the ice as we did, and theirs were every bit as good as ours, but we tried to maintain heavy pressure on them: I passed the puck to Weston, he passed it to Ignas, and he passed it back to Weston, in hopes of confusing the Rangers as to who had the puck. Weston made a slap shot, the goalie Johnson blocked it, but Curtiss got the rebound and did an admirable job of trying to stuff it in past Roeske, who lay in a heap on the ice while Ignas, Weston and I crowded around the goalie until the referee blew the puck dead. My stomach suddenly filled with gas that demanded to be released. I farted and nearly wept with relief.

Roeske looked up and said, "Dammit, who ripped one?"

"Whew!" Kursar exclaimed, skating away and fanning his face. Even the referee tried to pinch his nose discreetly as he retrieved the puck from Roeske.

Soon we were at the two-minute warning. Jacques had Ignas, Weston, Pavel, Curtiss and me on the ice. Barrie got control of the puck on the face-off in our own zone and we took turns passing it between ourselves as the Rangers tried to steal it away. Within seconds, Ignas, right by our net, tried to pass the puck to me but instead flipped it feebly to Kursar, who fired it past Fillo a moment before the end-of-game horn blew. New York Rangers 3—Bayporte Bullies 2.

Our locker room seemed as desolate as the Sahara. The equipment manager stuffed the sweated-through uniforms into trunks and made a final inspection of the lockers. A stadium janitor cleared away the last of our considerable debris, and the straggling sports reporters had departed after listening to Jacques LaPierre blame our loss on everyone but himself.

The final airport-bound bus sat rumbling outside the stadium as the first one neared its destination. I heard someone taking a shower in the stadium and discovered Barrie, letting the water pound his face and chest. After a few minutes I called out to him.

"Barrie, we better hurry up or the bus will leave without us."

"I'm almost done."

"Well, hurry the fuck up and we'll find a place to smoke up."

Soon we left the locker room. We passed by the equipment manager as he loaded the trunks of our filthy uniforms into a van that would take the funky clothing to be loaded onto a Canadian Airways 737 stocked with crap sandwiches and warm pop for our inflight consumption.

"I want a nice Canadian Comfort over ice," Barrie said, now dressed, his hands stuffed into the pockets of his parka, his hair still damp from his shower.

"Maybe they'll have something you like on the flight."

We reached the parking lot, but Barrie walked away, towards the stadium seats. Our driver stood by his bus, smoking a cigarette, apparently in no hurry to leave. So I went off with Barrie and said, "We need to make this quick." The house lights were down and I could scarcely see him in the darkness.

"Got a joint?" he asked as we sat side by side.

"Yeah, somewhere in here. Let me check." I felt surprised by how merry I sounded. As long as I did my best, I cared very little about wins and losses. Our productive season struck me as a trivial matter, even though everyone back in Bayporte bragged about it as if we had already won the Stanley Cup. Barrie, always a sore loser, could even be a sore winner when he wasn't the hero of the game.

"Dammit," he muttered as we finished the joint. "Lost another one."

On board the plane, we sat for more than an hour while the captain tried to get the OK for takeoff. Linda couldn't get us the little bottles of Canadian Comfort or steroids Barrie wanted, so he morosely curled up in his seat and tried to sleep. Some players got up and wandered around, half of them gingerly because of their aches and pains. I just sat like a zombie, wondering when we would get the hell out of the Big Apple.

Donny Bourdin, his handsome face rearranged, arrived stitched and bandaged. His ambulance pulled up well before takeoff. Stoned on painkillers, he sat drooling blood as a flight attendant pushed his wheelchair down the aisle. The doctor recommended seating him in first class, but Roderick Rainey, grossed out by the sight of Bourdin, insisted that some of the other Bullies carry him back to sit with the rest of us. Donny tried to talk but only managed goos and gahs.

I thought for a moment about Jacques' postgame comments to the media. "Clearly, the mistakes made by Bourdin and Ignas were detrimental to us, but we played poorly in general."

Jacques would almost certainly try to trade Bourdin soon and tell the reporters that it had nothing to do with what happened to the young man's face that day against the Rangers. Bourdin, too badly injured for the imminent postseason, would sit at home watching as the Bullies went after our first-ever Stanley Cup. He had merely become a bashed-in part that needed to be replaced, and Jacques would replace him promptly. I despised Jacques for being so aloof and detached, even though he needed to be that way in order to make the Bullies a winning NHL team.

"So," asked Linda Gee, "how is everything? Sorry I couldn't get you what you wanted."

She spoke to me but gazed at Barrie as he remain in a deep slumber. She lovingly dug her long fingernails into his thick wavy hair.

"He's tired and bored," I said. "He wants to go home and get ready for the playoffs."

She said nothing; she simply kept raking her nails through his hair. Barrie, a handsome man, had charisma and talent. I couldn't resist him, either, but my attraction to him was different from hers. Or maybe not; I wouldn't have been ashamed to admit being queer for him.

"Is he feeling all right?" she asked.

"Been better. We lost, you know."

"He is awesome," she said. "Does it bother him when you lose?"

"Certainly."

"Do you hate to lose, too?"

I grinned. "I get paid anyway." Then, "You adore him."

She smiled. "Yes."

"Why?"

She hardly hesitated to answer. "Because he is what a man should be. An ideal."

"And I'm not?"

"You're a real man. He's an ideal man." She went off to look after her other charges. Presently I had another visitor.

"So, tell me about the game. I missed it all," Snoop said.

"Gee, too bad for you."

"I'm serious. Quit dicking me around and tell me what happened so I can file my report."

"Really? You missed all of it?"

"Oh, I might've caught a minute or two, but I don't remember any of it." He eased himself into a seat next to me and looked at me for a minute or two. "So, tell me all about it."

"We lost, Snoop."

"Figures. That's all I really need to know. If I want details, I can just look over someone's shoulder when they file their story." Then, "Did the Paki really blow it?"

"Paki?"

"Warren said, 'That dumb fuckin' Paki cost us the game when he passed the puck to Kursar with two seconds left.'"

"Ignas didn't do it on purpose, and he's not a 'Paki.'"

Doctor Harri just then came towards us from the front of the aircraft. He had gotten very drunk because he hated to fly and inebriation minimized his discomfort. As he struggled towards us, he patted shoulders, offered consoling smiles and nearly fell on people as the aircraft hit small pockets of turbulence.

"Drunken fool," Snoop said. Doctor Harri heard him and frowned.

"Pay him no attention, Doctor," I said. "He's on the rag because we lost the game."

"I understand his disappointment," Doctor Harri said. "But a person should always mind his manners."

"Why?" Snoop asked.

"Because it's the right thing to do."

"Says who?"

"Powers greater than yourself say so."

Snoop smirked. "Do those powers speak to you personally?"

"Yes, they do. They would speak to you, too, if you would care to hear them."

"And what would they tell me? 'Go become a priest so you can molest little boys'?"

Doctor Harri shook his head the slightest bit and turned to look at me, as if I had an apology or explanation ready for Snoop's smart mouth. Then he sighed and turned to tell Denis Pilon that he had played an outstanding game and become a crucial part of the

Bayporte Bullies team. He got up and went down the aisle to say hello to other people.

"I despise him," Snoop said.

"He's a Christian. I thought you were one, too."

"I was, before I became an agnostic."

Harv Arthur sat down next to Snoop and me. "Hiya, fellas. You played a terrific game, Cross."

"Did he?" asked Snoop, taking out his voice recorder. "I need to talk to Jacques."

"He's drunk," Harv said. "That should be quite an interview. "How's Barrie?"

"Like he's ready to retire and have someone ghostwrite his bestselling autobiography."

Harv laughed. "He'll never retire."

"Yes he will," I said, "and I'll bet you'll be standing there, holding open the door for him to leave so you can wear the letter C on your jersey."

"I'm in no hurry to be the new captain. I'll get the job when I get it."

"Sooner rather than later, though, eh?" I paused. "Some people felt you should have gotten it this year."

He shrugged. "Well, I didn't get it."

"Doesn't that bug you?"

Harv shook his head. "I'll be the captain and be Barrie's replacement when Jacques says so. I guess I need more experience. Plus, I don't want to have any bad feelings with Barrie. We're great friends and he's still the star of the show. He deserves to be the captain."

"Do you really think so?"

"Absolutely. On the ice, we're competitors, but off the ice, we're great friends."

"Be honest, Harv. Do you think you're a better hockey player than Barrie?"

He took a deep breath and looked bemused. "I guess I do think I'm better than he is, but obviously Jacques doesn't see things that way, so I need to keep working hard and prove to Jacques that I should have Barrie's job."

"What if Jacques never feels that way?"

"Oh, he will. I guarantee you that. He will."

"But if he doesn't?" I persisted.

"Like I said, he will. No question there. It's just a matter of time."

"But what if Barrie is better than you, and he just stays and plays like he always has and your whole career turns out to be more of the same?"

Harv shook his head. "No way. Won't happen."

"Then how come you're still second line?"

"Like I said, that's Jacques' call. I wouldn't play the way Barrie did today, and when I'm on the first line I will do things differently."

"I see." I lay back and closed my eyes.

"What's *that* supposed to mean? Did you check the scoreboard at the end of the game? We lost, right?"

"I'm not totally convinced that our defeat was Barrie's fault."

"No? I think it's *always* the star's fault when the team loses."

"Hmm." I stretched out on my seat and felt wonderfully drowsy. "Whatever you say, guy." I closed my eyes and drifted off to sleep. In my dream I entered a boxing ring with a huge crowd cheering and flashbulbs bursting everywhere. In the ring, waiting for me, was Dolph Lundgren, the massive blond guy from one of the *Rocky* movies. He and I both wore trunks and gloves, which meant, presumably, that I had to fight him. I was scared to death that he would beat the shit out of me, but the crowd grew louder and louder, and their noise woke me up. Right away I heard the raised voices of Pavel and Jimmie Gish, who were carrying on about something. Pavel, still mentally and emotionally in Madison Square Garden, sometimes picked a verbal postgame fight just to expend his own aggressive energies.

Pavel had glided off the ice and sat still while the doctors did what they could for him, which meant doping him up enough to make the pain tolerable. The next day he would be X-rayed at the hospital for breaks, and he would tell them he felt no pain even if his agony were excruciating. To Pavel, complaining of pain was for pussies.

Gish knew that, according to Pavel, the Bullies' loss to a significantly weaker team was ultimately the fault of the coaching staff, especially Jimmie Gish. Gish pondered his options: he could simply stand there and endure the verbal abuse of this behemoth, who would surely and happily mock Gish's manliness, intelligence and honor; or he could talk back to Pavel despite how terrifying such an experience might be.

"Fock you man!" Pavel screamed. "All you talk about is numbers and statistics. I'm sick of you! You say it's a business but I'm sick of that, too."

"It *is* a business. You are businessmen—"

"Business? Fuck you! We are hockey players. You don't own us. I play hockey my best, but when the game is over and I'm tired, it must be more about scores and money. I can make money another way. Hockey is my life. It is more than business."

"You have a job. You play hockey for us."

"You hear what I just say?" Pavel yelled. They could probably hear him on the ground 30,000 feet below.

"You disagree with everything we say! If we say it's this, you say it's something else. You want us on the ice to be strangers pretending to be a team! Bullshit!"

Gish looked around. Onboard an aircraft, he had few escape options.

"I say this to you." Pavel stuck his long, thick finger in Gish's face. "You and Jacques and all the other big shots are focking assholes! You know nothing about hockey and could not play if you tried. You will win because of us, but what will it mean? Hey? Tell me!"

"To hell with this noise. I don't have to stand here and listen to it." Gish tried to get past Pavel.

"Like fock you don't, you focking asshole!" Pavel yelled, grabbing at Gish's collar. Gish pulled away and scrambled off to tell Jacques about this confrontation.

"Focking assholes!" Pavel screamed at the terrified departing coach. "Coaches can suck my cock!" He pointed his finger around, meaning to include all of his teammates, and said, "You too! You're all focking assholes! You can suck my cock, too!"

Maybe, I thought, the big guy had a point about us.

The big jet airliner banked right over downtown Bayporte and I looked out the window, afraid the aircraft would crash onto the Nu West Sports Building. I sat straight up and shook Barrie's shoulder. The jet began losing altitude as it approached Bayporte International Airport, and I recognized the clutch of new, shiny, unsightly buildings besotting downtown. Bayporte, a "new" Canadian major city, celebrated its present, eagerly anticipated its future and tried to forget its past. (Although who could think of any reason to be ashamed of Bayporte's past?)

Hundreds of well-wishers waited for us at the Canadian Airways terminal. To avoid them, Barrie and I used one of the "special" exits for those who wished to make themselves unavailable to adoring masses. Minutes later, we walked out of the main terminal, both of us feeling like Michael J. Fox the time we saw him sneaking out of the airport on Christmas Eve, head down, tote bag slung over his shoulder, feet working fast.

"You played some awesome hockey, Barrie," the valet attendant said as we gave him our tickets. "It's a shame you guys lost anyway."

Barrie shrugged. "Win some, lose some, eh?"

The attendant frowned, not altogether in concurrence with Barrie's wisdom, and phoned down to get Barrie's car. Soon, other people stood in line behind us, eager to drive home. One of those people, a middle-aged man in a Bullies warmup jacket, tapped Barrie's shoulder.

"Barrie? Barrie Weston?" The man pumped Weston's hand like a cop trying to force a dime bag of cocaine from a dealer's grip. "I'm Tommy Roberts. We have a few mutual friends." He sounded breathless.

"Do we?" Weston's eyes and smile looked old and tired.

"Yes we do! Vic and Emily Galbraith. I saw them not long ago. I come down to Bayporte sometimes. I'm in the mining business, you know."

Vic and Emily were Barrie's former parents-in-law.

"That's nice," Barrie muttered, stifling a yawn. "How are they?"

"Great, terrific," said the man, his head bobbing. "Saw your ex, too, and the little boy. My, he looks just like you. You should've had some more rugrats."

Barrie nodded the slightest bit, his eyelids halfway down. He looked the way I did moments before I vomited.

"Hey, guy," I said to the man gushing all over Barrie, "why don't you just piss off and leave us alone?"

The man turned to me, his smile still wide but hid Adam's apple now bobbing with fear. "Who the fuck are *you*?"

"I'm Barrie's teammate and bodyguard. Piss off or you'll get my foot up your ass. Understand?"

"You threatening me?" he asked, his smile now a sneer.

Barrie's car arrived just then. He still seemed disoriented, so I gave him a nudge and he stumbled towards his vehicle. My car waited directly behind his, so I turned around, gave a brisk backhanded slap to the face of the man who had been pestering Barrie, and got into my own car. When Barrie's car remained motionless, I got out and discovered him doubled over and gasping for air.

With the valet's assistance, I carried Barrie to my own car. The valet drove off to return Barrie's vehicle to the lot and I drove my teammate home. A few times we stopped so he could retch a brown river of toxins onto the pavement a few inches from my car. By the time we reached the endless rows of flimsy, boxy apartment complexes that had become Bayporte's most envied neighborhood, Barrie felt vastly better and insisted that I come in for a few minutes.

"You may meet somebody nice here. Most of the women are notoriously easy," he said.

At Barrie's door, his best friend and longtime companion, Babaloo, met us with joyful barks and forepaws at our groins. An oversize beige dog of indeterminate pedigree, Babaloo became Barrie's roommate after Jaylene Weston left her husband.

"Come on, Babaloo, get away from us," Barrie commanded. But Babaloo continued to dance and jump around us, his spittle flying and nails clicking.

Barrie went into his bedroom to change, and I went looking around his apartment. He lived in an oversized one-bedroom unit, fairly typical of the kind they built for newly divorced, overpaid men who still only half-believed their marriages had ended. The furniture, expensive but mismatched, already looked worn and lumpy despite being scarcely a year old. Stains as bold as Rorschach blots discolored the carpeting, and piles of dried dog feces sat here and there like little land mines.

Barrie had changed into a light-blue Oxford shirt, pleated khaki slacks and brown loafers. He looked like one of those affluent, semiretired West Shore guys he probably expected to become one day.

I thought of driving out to Laurel's house but decided against it and promised myself a good night's sleep. I thought about my performance on the ice this season and concluded that I had done well. Despite our loss to the Rangers, I had scored two goals, made one assist and stolen the puck of a couple of key occasions. Jacques couldn't complain about me. I resolved to be more diplomatic and less selfish, both on and off the ice.

"You played an outstanding game today," I said to Barrie.

"Outstanding wasn't good enough," he said. "We lost, in case you didn't notice."

"Don't blame yourself. We made our share of mistakes. Still, we're going all the way this year, and everyone knows it."

"Doesn't matter. My job out there is to win hockey games. If we lose, I haven't done my job."

"You sound like Vince Lombardi," I said.

"I sound like Jacques." Barrie paused. "For a little while, I thought Harv was infallible. He's got size and strength, he does his best and works hard, but he's too dumb to become great. Have you noticed that?"

"I don't know if he's dumb, but I'll take your word for it. He's a team player."

"So am I. But he and I aren't on the same team, if you ask me."

"If you ask me, Barrie, we are not the team. Jacques, Roderick and

Warren are the team. We're just the guys wearing the jerseys. Tell me, which superstar hates us the most?"

Barrie smiled. "Sid the Kid. We have his number."

"And do you know why? It's because Jacques has been studying Sid's performances so closely."

"So what?"

"It's just that you think you're a great and unique hockey player. Jacques doesn't think so. He thinks you're a valuable piece of equipment just like Sid the Kid. When you guys start to get old and tired, they'll just get new Barries and Sids."

"No. Wrong." Barrie snarled. "Completely wrong. You're just mad because Jacques has been coming down on you about the steroids. He's making you the scapegoat."

"Yeah, and that's been bugging me lately."

"Do you know what your problem is?" Barrie asked. "You let the world and its bullshit get to you. That's a serious problem for a person to have. I used to have that problem, but I overcame it."

"How did you do that?" I asked as Babaloo came over to lick my face and have me scratch his stomach.

"You just make up your mind that you aren't going to let the bastards grind you down. When I was a little kid, my mum and dad took me in to have my appendix removed. But they were smart enough not to tell me anything, except that we were going to the doctor. They kept me from yelling and screaming over having to have surgery and go into the hospital. But the weird thing was, they were quiet and somber, so I knew it was something serious, and I was terrified, but I pretended everything was OK. Do you understand?"

I said yes. I'd seen a few doctors and hospitals during my childhood.

"I still played little tough guy," Barrie went on, "even when they brought me into the OR and the doctors were all business and they put me to sleep, I didn't let on for a moment that I was the least bit afraid. Do you see my point? Take it all in stride, don't ever let them see you sweat or cry. That's my way."

I shook my head. "I couldn't do that, Barrie. I'm not you. When I went in for my surgery, I carried on like the little kid I was, throwing temper tantrums and getting everyone worked up."

"Did it make any difference? Did the doctor say, 'Oh, the poor little lad! We can't cut him open'? Of course not. They did what they had to do. So don't fight it."

I shrugged and nodded. "Easier said than done."

"Do you know why I love playing hockey?" Barrie asked. "It's simple, man. Just us and the puck, and the game. It has nothing to do with anything else that is happening in the world, and its meaninglessness is what turns me on. The world's problems will still be there once the game is over, but while the game is on, we say, 'Fuck the chaos and misery; let's drop the puck and have some fun.'"

I frowned a bit and nodded. "I suppose that's what motivates all of us to play in the first place. And that's what motivates the fans to come out."

Barrie smiled. "Exactly. I'm glad we agree on something. That doesn't happen too often these days."

"But do you still get that much pleasure from playing hockey?"

"I'm not sure I had that much fun a few seasons ago, when we sucked. Now that we're headed for the postseason, I feel like a little kid again." He looked at me, his eyes glittering with emotion. "I want to hoist that Cup in the air and wear that championship ring, Cross. I want it more than anything, now that I know it's really possible. I don't know how long the Bullies will play this well, or how long we'll all stay together as a team, especially if some of us start failing piss tests and lose our jobs. We need to win the Cup this year or next year, or it will never happen."

"You're completely and totally into winning," I said. "Doesn't that seem immoral to you?"

"It seems virtuous. If you go out there to win, and you do win, that's a good thing."

"What matters is the game, Barrie. The winning or losing is a trivial matter; win this one, lose that one, who gives a shit? The point is playing, not winning or losing."

"No way. Not to me."

We said nothing more. I just kept petting Babaloo and considering what Barrie had just told me. Then I got up and started to think about leaving. "I suppose we listen to whoever has the opinion we value most. I'm not sure that I think my opinion is the most accurate, but my opinion is that I'm quite a good hockey player, and that opinion appeals to me a great deal."

Barrie shrugged, as he always did when a conversation bored him and he was ready to move on to other things. He summoned Babaloo and started scratching the dog's stomach as I walked over to the front door. "See you when I see you," I said.

"Yeah," he muttered as he petted his dog. Then he started talking, softly but passionately, to Babaloo.

8

When my iPhone rang in the morning, I couldn't figure out anything and it rang a dozen times or more before I answered it.

"Coach LaPierre wants to see you at eleven this morning in his office," said Jacques' secretary.

"What if *I* don't wanna see *him?*"

"Excuse me?"

"Nevermind. Tell him I'll get to his office after I have my coffee and drop a deuce."

"Excuse me?"

"I'll be there," I said. Office meetings were scary things, and I knew this one would be, too. I filled the bathtub, got in and soaked for close to an hour. Then I drove over to the skyscraper and stood at the secretary's desk, fifteen minutes early.

"How's it goin'?" I asked her.

"It's going fine," she said, reading an E.L. James novel.

"Do you like those books? I can't get into those chick-lit novels. I like Harry Potter novels. I guess that's because I'm a thirteen-year-old boy at heart."

She ignored me. Presently the phone rang, and she answered it. "You may go into see him now." Then she continued reading her book.

I walked down the long hallway towards Jacques' office and observed, right away, that all the other offices were unoccupied. I heard no voices and saw no one walking to or from the washrooms or other offices. The place was just too damn quiet. Jacques' secretary did not look at me as she opened the door to the big man's office and I beheld a who's-who of NHL power and importance.

Jacques sat at one end of his large desk. Surrounding him were Roderick Rainey, Warren Gotch and Ted Haibeck, the man in charge of NHL internal affairs. The only one I didn't recognize was a fortysomething man brown hair and a goatee. Unlike the others, he wore a poorly fitting, garish sports jacket. For a moment, I felt surprised and disappointed that the American president and Canadian prime minister weren't there, too.

Confused and alarmed, I looked closely at the faces in the office. Jacques had Roderick Rainey on his right and Warren Gotch on his left. In the utter silence, I could hear Warren's fingers tapping on the desk as if he were a jazz drummer banging on the skins. Gotcha had guzzled a pot of coffee in preparation for a long and difficult day. Next to him sat Ted Haibeck, the man in charge of internal affairs and security for the NHL.

When had I last seen Roderick, Jacques, Warren and Haibeck in the same room? Never, especially not Haibeck, a ten-year veteran of the RCMP's special investigations unit; he normally sent his assistants to do his dirty work. His job consisted mainly of surveillance of players and investigations of their alleged misconduct.

Jacques made quick, cursory introductions and sorted through some computer printouts laid out before him. Then he isolated one and perused it as if it contained the answer to the question, "Who *really* killed JFK?"

"Chris," he said at last as he stared at the printout, "where were you on Wednesday night until early Thursday morning?"

"Hey?" I wouldn't be worth much on the witness stand in a court of law.

"On last Wednesday night, where were you?" The printout remained in his hands. He looked in my direction but still refused to make eye contact with me.

I gazed around the room and observed Thornton Rainey's absence. On last Wednesday night, I had been ravishing Thornton's fiancée. Instead of having Thornton here this morning, we had a man named House, the Bullies' attorney and a close personal friend of the Raineys. A corpulent, bald young man, he wheezed quite audibly and sweated profusely. His three chins quivered with each breath.

"I don't recall my whereabouts," I told them, "but you clearly do. Why do you ask?"

"Because we must know," Warren Gotch said, tapping the tabletop. As the general manager, and thus the equal of every man in this room, he had the right to speak whenever he wished to do so. I hoped he hadn't taken some uppers along with his coffee; such a combination would make him as irrational as a skid-row speed freak.

"Tell me what I have done wrong," I said, looking around at all their faces.

"You better cooperate, sir," said Ted Haibeck. *Sir*. He sounded like one of my high school teachers whenever I misbehaved. I smirked a bit, thinking of those long-gone days, and my smirk hardly eased the anxiety in the room.

"If you already have the answers, why are you asking me these questions?"

"We want you to have your say before we go any farther," Jacques told me.

"It seems like you've already made up your minds," I said.

"You need to cooperate with us fully," Warren Gotch added, as if negotiating how many goodies I would get in my next contract. His tabletop-tapping grew louder and faster. I suddenly knew I was up shit creek without a paddle.

I looked down and stared at the tabletop. If all else fails, shut the fuck up. Nobody said anything for a couple of minutes.

Finally, Gotcha said, "Go ahead, Mr. Hutsch."

The bulky man in the ugly sports coat stood up and walked over to Jacques and Haibeck. From my perspective, he stood in the space behind both men, as if seeking their protection from me, the way I had hidden behind my bodyguards when schoolyard punks wanted to pummel me. Hutsch looked down at his own documents and ran a hand through his goatee. His face tightened in disgust as he scanned the paper, as if they contained words I had spoken and deeds I had done, that he found reprehensible. A hardened, pugnacious man, Hutsch would probably prefer to punch me out than discuss my infractions.

"My name is Aaron Hutsch. I am an undercover officer for the Bayporte police. I also work for Mr. Haibeck, looking into issues of player misconduct."

Warren Gotch's head turned to and fro, as if in time to a favorite song. He stopped tapping on the tabletop for a moment and cocked his head in Hutsch's direction, knowing what the man had to say beforehand.

"Some time ago," Hutsch continued, "Mr. Haibeck contacted me about doing surveillance on Christopher Crossley, a player for the Bayporte Bullies."

Just then I recalled Hutsch's rugged face and deep voice. He had phoned me once to ask me to make do an unsalaried meet-and-greet at some fundraising function for the families of fallen cops. I spent much of the evening at his side. We didn't say much to each other, but now he had plenty to say about me. What an ingrate.

"I followed him from the time that Mr. Haibeck contacted me until the following Friday, when Mr. Crossley boarded a flight to New York."

"Well...?" Warren Gotch looked at me.

"He's right," I said. "I flew to New York. I had a nice flight."

Gotcha glared at me for a few moments, then said, "Go ahead, Mr. Hutsch." He started drumming on the tabletop again. I sighed and sat back.

"I will read from my notes," said Hutsch, speaking slowly and clearly. "On Monday morning, I began following Mr. Crossley to Roy's Pancake House where he met several other men…"

"Who?" I blurted out. "Tell us who the men were."

"I don't know who they were," he said.

"Really? Didn't you recognize any of them?" I asked, incredulous. "Were they short or tall, fat or skinny, black or white…?"

"No, I did not note their sizes." His eyes darted from me to Warren Gotch.

Gotcha sneered at me. "Crossley, what are you up to?"

"I'm just trying to make sure that this guy knows what he's talking about," I said.

"We've already established his reliability," Warren said. "Continue, Aaron."

"At the restaurant, the men, including Mr. Crossley, unloaded several shotguns and other kinds of hunting equipment from one vehicle and then put those items into a large vehicle commonly known as a Hummer. Then they all got into the Hummer and headed north on the Western Canada Highway into the wilderness. I assumed they would be shooting at wildlife and I didn't want them to know that an officer of the law was following them."

"Too bad for you," I said. "You missed out on a good time."

"Quiet!" Gotcha pounded on the tabletop, his face red and his breathing hard.

"I remained in the parking lot of the pancake house until the men returned," Hutsch said. He glanced from Haibeck to Gotcha, who looked at me and then at each other.

"When Mr. Crossley and the others got back, Mr. Crossley got into his vehicle and headed immediately to a house near downtown Bayporte, where a party was occurring. I naturally did not attempt to enter the premises but observed from the street."

"What was the address of that house?" I asked.

"You tell us," he retorted. "You were there, carrying on."

"But you're supposed to be a professional. You need to know these things," I said.

"I don't know the address," Hutsch said, snarling.

"Mr. Crossley," said Ted Haibeck, gripping Warren Gotch's forearm so that Gotcha wouldn't leap to his feet and start screaming. "Please respect the seriousness of this meeting and do not be flippant."

I nodded and pursed my lips. Then I closed my eyes and rested my chin on the heel of my hand.

"Continue, Aaron," Haibeck said.

He did just that, being careful to avoid mentioning anything about anyone except me. "I observed Mr. Crossley sharing a marijuana cigarette with another male whose name I did not know." He meant Barrie Weston, one of the most famous people in Canadian sports history.

"How do you know it wasn't just a regular tobacco cigarette?" asked Warren Gotch.

"Because people usually don't pass tobacco cigarettes back and forth and smoke those cigarettes until they're tiny."

"Anything else?" Gotch asked him.

"Marijuana smokers," Hutsch said with a sneer, as if talking about terrorists, faggots or pedophiles, "take short, aggressive puffs and hold the smoke in. That's what they were doing."

Everyone stayed quiet for a few moments, perhaps to allow me to say something in my own defense or to get myself into deeper trouble. I stayed silent but boiled with rage.

"Soon after I observed Mr. Crossley smoking marijuana—"

"Do you know it was pot, you stupid fat fuck?" I screamed, jumping up. "*You fuckin' goof!*"

"Don't speak to *me* that way!" Hutsch hollered, taking a step towards me, his hands balled into fists. I started to stand up, too, and Hutsch faltered a bit and looked around to see who would side with him. Haibeck spoke up.

"Mr. Crossley, do not be offended by what Mr. Hutsch says during this meeting. He is simply doing his job, which is to present information as he has acquired it. But you must understand that we hired him because of his considerable competency as an officer of the law. We will not accept profanity or other kinds of disparaging language."

"Why don't you just have him Taser me to death right now?"

"Again, Mr. Crossley, your flippancy serves no good purpose. These are serious matters and you need to cooperate fully. Proceed, Mr. Hutsch."

The big cop and Warren Gotch exchanged glances. Gotcha gave him a smile and nod.

"Well, soon after seeing Mr. Crossley consume cannabis, I terminated my surveillance for the night. I caught up with him again the following afternoon as he drove to the Nu West Sports Building for a couple of hours. After departing Nu West Sports, he drove to the Heritage Apartments, where he spent the night."

"Can you tell us," Gotcha asked, tapping his fingers and squirming in his seat while shooting me a dirty look, "in which suite Mr.

Crossley spent that night?"

"Yessir. It was sixteen-oh-one. The resident's name is—"

"Irrelevant," said House, the Raineys' attorney, speaking for the first time in this meeting. "The person's name doesn't matter."

Hutsch looked confused. His mouth was already rounded to say *Monique.* He continued, but more tentatively now, after having been interrupted and losing his place. "Crossley spends many nights there," he said, looking from Gotcha to Haibeck and back again, fearing that he had said more than he should have.

"Bastards," I said, and the word, like a racquetball, bounced off the walls, then off the heads of these men. After a few moments, the stunned silence grew tedious and the talk resumed.

"In the early hours," Hutsch said after clearing his throat, "I left the apartment building and drove to Mr. Crossley's house. I searched the premises and found pornographic videos and bottles of liquid that appeared to be performance-enhancing drugs."

"Those porno videos are collector's items," I said.

They ignored me.

These King Shits of the NHL had gathered here to crucify me, and I was a fool to think I could defend myself against them. Even Haibeck had flown in from back east to ream me about screwing Thornton's bride-to-be. Their main grievance against me, I could see now, was my relationship with Monique; filling my body with steroids and human growth hormone gave them an excuse to do me in. Since I had no way of defending myself against them, I sat back and relaxed as they charged, tried, convicted and hanged me.

"The next night," Hutsch said with a victorious air, "I once again followed Mr. Crossley. This time he visited the home of Simon Kwan, a prominent broadcaster and peace activist but also a suspected dealer in controlled substances."

"You sneaky little monkey," I said.

"While Mr. Crossley was in Mr. Kwan's residence, I searched the former's vehicle and discovered two packages of human growth hormone pills which Mr. Crossley possessed illegally. Mr. Gotch has the pictures."

Gotcha held up the digital images for all to see. He swallowed hard and used both hands to hold the exhibits, as if the images were too heavy for him.

The big cop went on about what else I had done. He talked about the Igloo but insisted that he recognized no one there but Laurel and me. He drove behind us out to Whitley after the Igloo, and followed me out there again later that week. "The woman's name is Laurel English, and she resides on a large parcel of land. She also resides there with an Indian male but I am unclear about the nature of their relationship."

"I hear they're getting it on," I said.

Warren Gotch snarled at me. Everybody else let my remark pass by.

Hutsch concluded with my flight to New York and said nothing more. He returned to his seat, gathered up his documents Gotcha thanked him and Hutsch exited the room.

"What do you have to say about all this?" Gotcha asked me.

"I think you're the most uptight bunch of assholes I've ever met."

"You freaking idiot!" He jumped to his feet as his face went every color of rage. "You're nothing but a hockey player! You'll be gone soon and another guy will have your job! Just who the hell do you think you are?"

I shrugged and sat there, silent.

"Do you know *why* you're in the NHL?" he demanded. "You're in the NHL because we"—he gestured around at the roomful of heavies—"let you be here. *We* are under no obligation to *you*, but *you* are obligated to *us*, and there are tens of millions of hockey fans everywhere who see things the same as we do."

"Those tens of millions of fans seem pretty happy with me," I said, feeling a little more relaxed.

"Excuse me?" He nearly spat out the words and wiped his lips with the sleeve of his suit coat. His lips curved into a malicious little smile. "You're so damned smug, Crossley. You're trash from the wrong side of town. We took you in, gave you a good job, paid you well. Have you ever looked at your contract? Good money, eh? Go try to get *that* kind of money selling cars or real estate, or by standing at the door of some nightclub, shaking hands and kissing asses. You'll learn quickly enough that people will not give a damn about you once you've stopped wearing a Bullies uniform."

I simply looked at the livid general manager and waited for him to continue.

He held up a copy of my contract. "Can you read this? Probably not." Gotcha had a point; I honestly couldn't read an entire contract, even when my agent went through it with me. "If you *could* read it, Crossley, you would learn that you work for us, we don't work for you. You are our property. You can't even take a crap without our permission. That is why we have paid you so much money. It isn't because you're happy and handsome and a delight to your friends."

Ted Haibeck grabbed Gotcha, who had started to rise, and forced him to sit. Warren sank back and relaxed a bit, after taking a moment or two to glare at me.

"Have you anything to say at this point?" Haibeck asked me.

"Nope."

Jacques began looking through the documents before him. He

chose one and studied it for several moments, the way Gotcha did when negotiating contracts, pretending that the paper in his hands contained data that severely undermined the opponent's case.

"Chris," he finally said, "you've been in my office for private meetings during your years with the Bullies. Isn't that so?"

"Yes."

"Do you recall what we said to each other during those meetings?"

"Mainly you said that I had an attitude problem."

"Attitude problem." Jacques' mouth worked a bit, as a vintner might orally swirl wine with a questionable bouquet. "I believe, Chris, that you are a good forward. You may be one of the best in the NHL. You are certainly a capable hockey player, but so is everyone else on our team."

"I agree," I said.

"But being a member of the team requires dedication, devotion, discipline and emotional maturity. Each player must give as well as take."

"And you think I have been taking more than giving?" I asked.

"Don't you? It seems to me that you must adhere to the rules that have existed ever since the league began. Those people have worked very hard to set those rules. You cannot come in and do as you please, with disregard for the way things have always been done."

My eyes narrowed. "Jacques, you people have taken a sport and made it into a corporation. You're all after the almighty buck. You sit there in your two-thousand-dollar suits and fart into silk underwear. You have never played hockey or done any other kind of respectable work, then you start giving me shit about how I do my job."

Jacques sighed and looked at some more documents. "Warren is right; you *are* smug. In fact, I know far more about you than you suspect. We like to know who plays for us." He went through his documents and withdrew what I recognized as the results of a battery of psychological tests that all Bullies had to take.

"According to these tests," he said, "you are an above-average achiever who resists help from others. We believe you have few, if any, close friends or significant others. You are a liability to the

Bullies for the same reasons you are an asset. You become exasperated when you cannot control all aspects of your life and your exasperation leads you to attempt to destroy everything you cannot control." He paused and looked at me. "Do you understand? We must control our control freaks."

"Maybe I need shock treatments."

"Again, don't be flippant. You say you resent my aloofness and detachment, but my job requires me to have such qualities. I must do my job without emotional involvement. You, however, seem unwilling to do this. You will not place the rules above your own agenda."

I hung my head low, unable to escape from this predicament. "You insist on controlling my life without giving a damn about me as a person. The two don't separate; I'm not a robot, and it terrifies me that you think I am a robot or should act like one. You seem to think it's OK for me to have no human relationship with you people who 'own' me. You own me but you don't want to know me or care about me. How am I supposed to feel about that?"

Jacques just looked at me. Finally, he said, "I acknowledge your objections to me and the way I run this hockey team. But there is no onus on me to have a personal relationship with you or to be your friend. You have a job to do for us—to play hockey—and your personal life is another matter altogether. You and I have our personal differences, but you seem unable to able to cope with this fact. I am here to win hockey games, not to counsel troubled souls. You must not continue to question my authority. Dislike me if you want, but you must respect me."

"Jacques, be serious. You can't just tell people to respect you. As a hockey coach, you are the very best, but you apparently believe that your skill as a coach means you are a saint." I took a breath and tried to relax. My voice had been getting loud and strained.

"You seem to believe that there is something immoral or corrupt in winning, be it in hockey or life in general," Jacques said, doing his best to hide his contempt for what I had just said. "Winning is why we're here. In order to win, we must be responsible and make sacrifices; if we fail to do those things, we will lose. This attitude is what has made the Bullies one of the finest teams in the NHL.

Everyone fears and respects us. We adhere to the rules, and we win. You seem unwilling to do what is necessary."

"If your odious attitude is what we need to win, then I don't mind losing. But if you think you're right and I'm wrong, you're all damn fools." I said nothing more and waited for whatever would happen next. But I felt gratified to speak my mind to these men.

"I am afraid," Jacques said, his face and voice expressionless, "that you must do your philosophizing and navel-gazing at someone else's expense. You are making something complicated which is actually very straightforward. To have a winning organization of any kind, people within that organization must adhere to a set of rules. You, however, have decided to follow your own agenda, and that is unacceptable. Therefore, we have no use for you." He went through more documents and placed some of them into a manila folder, which he placed on a corner of his desk. He did so without speaking and everyone stayed silent and motionless.

Ted Haibeck withdrew a sheet of paper from his coat pocket, read it and frowned at me. "When we first learned of the serious charges against you—"

I laughed. "What charges? All we've heard so far was the activities of a fat fuck who's been following me around."

"Mr. Crossley, you are not on trial. There is no judge or jury. This is just a meeting about the private conduct of a hockey player, and how his conduct is unacceptable to us."

"You still refuse to specify the nature of my misconduct," I pointed out.

"Using steroids," Haibeck said.

"You've no proof of that. What else you got?"

"The young lady," Haibeck said. Roderick Rainey's future sister-in-law. Rainey just sat there, blank faced, his mind perhaps a hundred miles away.

"Monique?" I asked, speaking the forbidden name. "She's not a minor, and she's not even married, yet."

They all grimaced.

"Look," I continued, "I don't know why you seem to be so enraged by me. What have I done? Why are Ted Haibeck and

Roderick Rainey here for this confrontation? If this is about steroids—"

"It certainly *is* about steroids," Warren Gotch said.

"Well, I'm sure that guys throughout the NHL use steroids. The top players in the league. How do you think they got to be so good? Just through diet and exercise? As for Monique, she's not even married—"

"That is irrelevant," Haibeck said. "We are interested only in *your* transgressions."

"How come you guys are picking on me?" I implored, feeling a catch in my throat. I hadn't wept in front of other adults since my father's funeral and didn't want to break down now.

"You deserve to be picked on!" Warren Gotch yelled, shaking his fist. "You were observed committing infractions that merit suspension, and that suspension started a couple of hours ago." He fashioned my contract into a clumsy ball, then placed it on the table in front of himself as if the little wad of paper were a phone book he'd just muscled apart. "You're history."

House, the lawyer, smoothed out the slimy ball of paper, folded it and slipped it into his jacket pocket. Then he pushed a form towards me.

"Please sign this document, Mr. Crossley. It terminates your involvement with the Bullies. We would like to move ahead with this matter as fast as possible and handle it quietly. We're sure you want that, too."

"You can't do this to me!"

"It's a done deal, guy," Gotcha said, tapping his fingers against the table top in a kind of digital victory dance. "Also, you should be aware that the police have plenty of intelligence on you. If you have a Plan B in terms of your career and life, you should put it into action immediately."

I made an obscene finger gesture at him and said, "You son of a bitch! You know that all the other guys on the team have been doing worse things than I have, yet you're fucking *me* over. You just want to get rid of me for your own personal reasons."

"Mr. Crossley." Haibeck's voice sounded as cold as any killer's.

"It's unfortunate that you feel you're being singled out for persecution, but you should have thought about the consequences before you started using those substances. When we first became aware of the allegations against you, we wanted to ensure that you received due process. When we believed it was prudent to do so, we initiated an investigation concerning those allegations."

Haibeck said more, but I tuned him out. I felt nauseous and lightheaded, and wondered if I would need some assistance leaving the office once this meeting ended. After a minute or two, I felt slightly better and started considering things with more lucidity.

"The commissioner has made a statement that I want to read." The ex-Mountie proceeded: 'As commissioner of this league, I have the job of protecting the league from dangers within and without. We have judged your case exclusively on its merits. Our position is to resolve all conflicts and disputes if we can do so internally, rather than through the courts, police and so on. Ultimately, however, we must think of the league first, and to jettison those who attempt to compromise the integrity of the game, and to do so as quickly and quietly as possible.'"

I nodded, accepting the craziness of this morning's meeting. It all seemed sadly comical. I sat there and tried to talk sense to men who believed their own lies. They had no desire to respect the truth or do the right thing. They simply wanted to make everything convenient for themselves, and since they ran the entire league, they could, in effect, say to me, "Crossley, there is bad press going around about steroids in hockey, and we need to show the world that we're taking this matter seriously, so we're going to make you the fall guy because we're big and powerful. You can't defend yourself against us, so you should just walk away and find something else to do with the rest of your life."

I signed the form and slid it back to House. He smiled, and his chins jiggled. "Although you may not believe it right now," he said, "you have done the right thing..."

Suddenly I felt a wonderful sense of liberation. I had won my freedom, even if I had lost my fight. My shoulders and back felt lighter, as if the monkey clinging to my back had just scampered away. I looked with childlike glee around this big, imposing office and these ruthless, powerful men populating it, knowing that now I sat here as a guest or a fan, not as a victim or wayward employee. No longer did I feel any need to try to control the world I lived in; I simply had to sit back and be myself. The game, the bullshit, had ended; no longer would I feel defeat, shame or failure as a cog in the corporate machine. The game had never been on ice, anyway; it had always been up here, in Jacques' office. I hadn't been fired, nor had I quit; I had simply disappeared, as insubstantial as a puff of smoke. The phonies and fakers, and movers and shakers, could have it all. From now I was free just to be myself, to leave that office and take the elevator downstairs and get into my car. Then I would speed out there to Whitley and ask Laurel to let me spend the rest of my life with her. At my age, I had finally become my own man; I could do my own thing.

"As of noon, Pacific Standard Time," read Ted Haibeck, "you are suspended from playing in the National Hockey League. Your Contract is no longer valid and this office deems that disbursements, financial or otherwise, will be made by the Bayporte Bullies."

I didn't feel totally convinced that they wanted to get rid of me personally. Maybe my contract troubled them more; I just happened to be the body chained to it. They would be better off without me and my syringes and pills and backtalk. Once the commissioner and these other heavies got me into Jacques' office and had their say, they could consider me one fewer pain in their corporate ass. I couldn't fight them in the courts. This meeting happened so that they could explain such things to me, and I wondered why they even bothered. These men surely knew they could rid themselves of me, or anyone else, by saying that the player in question just wasn't a good fit for their organization. Who had the balls to fight them? My only option was to give in. I would look like a jackass in court, filing a lawsuit in the province of Great Elizabeth against the National Hockey League.

Ted Haibeck concluded reading from his document and looked at me as I stood up, strode to the door, opened it and took one last look at this gathering of smug men who had assembled here this morning just to give my gonads a few sharp cranks. I gave them my best sad smile and walked away.

The wind blew back my hair as I exited the Nu West Sports Building. Clayey clouds blew across the mostly bright sky. The cool wind felt good; I suddenly felt hungry, so I started to think of where I wanted to eat.

I stood on the sidewalk for a few moments, fiddling with the car keys in my pocket and   heard a voice behind me.

"Cross."

"Barrie," I replied, turning around. "You know I just came from a big meeting? Gotcha, Jacques, Rainey, Haibeck. Even Rainey's lawyer was there."

He nodded. We stayed silent for a minute or two.

"So," he said at last, "what happened?"

"They talked, I listened."

"And..?" Barrie asked.

"They know all about the juicing."

"Did they talk about me?"

I shook my head. "They didn't care about you. All the big guys were in that room and they were after me. Can you imagine? Fucking

Haibeck flew all the way out here just to hassle little ol' me! They kicked me off the team."

Barrie nodded. "I figured that would happen. Thanks for not dragging me into that whole mess."

"As of now, I'm no longer a Bully. You guys are going into the postseason without me. Can you handle it?"

He grinned. "Yeah, I think so."

"No Bourdin, either. He'll take a couple of months for his face to heal up."

"Don't need him, either. With me, Ignas, Pilon, Horton, Fillo...we'll do OK. Fuck, Harv Arthur is going to love this, because Jacques will move him up to first line now as your replacement." He looked at the ring finger on his left hand. "I wonder how that championship ring is going to look. Hope they don't fuck it up."

"I think I'm going to move out to the boonies for a few years," I said.

He smiled. "Say hi to Laurel for me."

"I'll do that."

Barrie reached into his jacket pocket and took out a puck. "Here's a little going-away present for you." He tossed it to me, and I caught it with one hand. I grinned at the very familiar autograph in grease pencil, then flung the puck into the sky and gave Barrie, and the world, my biggest and happiest laugh.

ABOUT THE AUTHOR

George Onstot has worked as an attack-dog agitator and a nightclub
emcee, but mostly he has been a flunky, toady and gofer.
He was born in San Francisco but has lived for some time near
Vancouver. Over the years he has written many novels and short
stories, and he is finally starting to publish some of them.

www.ingramcontent.com/pod-product-compliance
Lightning Source LLC
Chambersburg PA
CBHW062007170626
46813CB00001B/63